The Secret of the
SENTINEL ROCK

The Secret of the
SENTINEL ROCK

JUDITH SILVERTHORNE

Edited by Barbara Sapergia.
Cover images: "Teenage Girl" by Steve Evans / Getty Images. Landscape photo by Masterfile. painting of girl on rock by Debbie Edlin.
Interior Illustrations by Kay Parley.
Cover and book design by Duncan Campbell.
Printed and bound in Canada by Tri-Graphic Printing.

Library and Archives Canada Cataloguing in Publication

Silverthorne, Judith, 1953-
　　　　The secret of Sentinel Rock / Judith Silverthorne.

(From many peoples)
Edited by Barbara Sapergia.
ISBN 978-1-55050-386-9

I. Sapergia, Barbara, 1943-　II. Title.　III. Series.

PS8587.I2763S44 2007　　　jC813'.54　　　C2007-902252-9

10　9　8　7　6　5　4　3　2　1

2517 Victoria Ave.
Regina, Saskatchewan
Canada　S4P 0T2

Available in Canada & the US from
Fitzhenry & Whiteside
195 Allstate Parkway
Markham, ON,　L3R 4T8

The publisher gratefully acknowledges the financial support of its publishing program by: the Saskatchewan Arts Board, the Canada Council for the Arts, the Government of Canada through the Book Publishing Industry Development Program (BPIDP), the City of Regina Arts Commission, the Saskatchewan Cultural Industries Development Fund, Saskatchewan Culture Youth and Recreation, SaskCulture Inc., Saskatchewan Centennial 2005, Saskatchewan Lotteries, and the Lavonne Black Memorial Fund.

CHAPTER ONE

Something was beckoning her from outside, Emily could sense it. Turning her back on the chattering crowd, she squirmed on the scratchy couch in her grandmother's living room, and looked out the window at the farmyard and pasture beyond it. The sun was bright in the vivid spring sky. For the first time in days she felt the stirrings of energy and a need for adventure. Yet there was something more than that, something willing her to go outdoors.

For two weeks Emily, her parents, and other family members had kept vigil at her grandmother's hospital bedside as she lay in the final stages of a failing heart and old age. Near the end her Grandmother Renfrew hadn't known anybody. She'd died peacefully in her sleep early in the morning four days ago at the age of ninety-six.

Even though Emily had been surrounded by family and friends since the funeral, she still felt hollow and drained. All she could think about was not being able to talk with her grandmother ever again. Wondering if the emptiness would always be there, she glanced wistfully out the window. The sudden longing to be outside tugged at her again.

Then someone nudged her and a plate of sand-wiches appeared in front of her. She shook her head and mumbled, "No thanks."

"You should try to eat something."

Emily looked up to find her mother standing anx-iously over her.

"I'm just not hungry, Mom."

Kate Bradford pushed her daughter's dark hair away from her face and felt her forehead. "I hope you're not coming down with something. You look flushed. Maybe you should go upstairs and lie down."

Before Emily could reply, Aunt Liz called from across the room. Emily watched her mother hurry away and disappear amid the crowd of relatives and neighbours who had come for lunch after the funeral service. Every available seat was occupied, and many people were milling about from one small chatting group to another in the stifling room. Flowers saved from the church were everywhere, their scent overwhelming. Emily felt like she was suffocating in the confines of the old stone house.

Screak. She jumped when someone opened the nearby window. From outside she could hear the call of a meadowlark. A few moments later a refreshing breeze filtered through the warm room. The desire to head out the door and across the prairie was stronger than ever. Maybe she'd go out for a walk. Her parents would think she'd gone to lie down, and probably nobody else would notice she was missing.

She stood up and threaded her way through the people in the living room. Her father flashed her a smile as she passed. Agnes Barkley, a close neighbour, swept her into a boisterous embrace. Aunt Liz winked at her, saying nothing. She was paying attention to Emily's mother as she orchestrated the visitors towards food and seats.

In the kitchen Gerald Ferguson, who rented her grandmother's land, shook Emily's hand and told her how sorry he was that her grandmother was gone. She thanked him, wiping the dampness from her eyes, and managed to escape.

Once on the porch she was careful not to let the screen door slam behind her and slipped outside. From the moment she stepped onto the back stoop she felt compelled to head across the yard to the meadow.

Emily turned towards the back of the tall stone house, away from the windows where someone might spot her. She crawled through the barbed-wire fence into the pasture, being careful to tuck in her skirt so it wouldn't get caught or torn. Then she raced across the wide open grasslands. The wind whipped her skirt against her bare legs and seemed to whisk her sadness away.

What a glorious spring day. The smell of dry grass and sage wafted up to Emily as she ran over the uneven ground. It was exhilarating to be away from the gloom and solemnness of the mourners. Emily felt sure her grandmother would understand. She had loved the prairie as much as Emily did.

As if in agreement, a chorus of frogs ribbitted in a nearby willow thicket. Emily laughed as she ran, drawn along a path she'd often taken with her grandmother. A meadowlark flitted overhead as she turned towards a clump of budding poplar trees just over a slight rise to her right. She followed its flute-like call as it paused here and there along the edge of the bush, until it disappeared over the treetops. She was on the other side of the bluff now, and could no longer be seen from the house.

She decided to catch her breath, then head back. She'd come quite far and hated the fuss her parents always made when she went off on her own. They'd probably discover she was missing soon. Emily sighed, and scratched at her bare legs where stray wisps of dry weeds tickled them.

She stood up to go back, but hesitated. Something drew her on. Stepping around a large stone half hidden in the tangled grass, she continued along the edge of the bluff, following the well-worn path. She felt the slight strain on her legs as she gradually headed uphill. A few feet beyond the trees, she saw the familiar outcropping of rock where she and her grandmother had often stopped. Emily smiled, and instinctively knew this was where she needed to go. It was the perfect place to rest before heading back.

Bursting into a quick trot up the last few feet of the incline, Emily found herself overlooking a small valley with its rolling hills that stretched and melted into the horizon. In all her wanderings across her grandmother's property, this was her favourite spot. Emily caught her breath at the sight of all the crocuses that dotted the south side of the hillsides, delicate glimmers of lavender amongst the patches of reviving grass.

In the distance to her left she could once again see Grandmother Renfrew's stone house, where she'd spent every summer of her twelve years. The massive two-story structure lost its distinguished look from this far away. In fact, it seemed quite small and ordinary.

With a sense of urgency Emily sprinted to the large light-grey boulder. It stood like a sentinel, its flat passive face overlooking the coulees, with a funny hat-shaped slab jutting out over the uppermost part. Although her Grandmother Renfrew had been too old to scale the huge dolomite rock in the last few years of her life, Emily had often proceeded to the top, reporting back all the things that she saw.

Today from the base of the rock the black expanse of the Barkleys' summerfallowed field opposite her grandmother's yard made a sharp contrast to the greening pasture below. Each was outlined by long stretches of barbed-wire fence, with little stone piles at the corners. And in the distance to the southeast she could just make out the outlines of Glenavon's grain elevators dotting the skyline.

Excitement rose in Emily as she circled the rock. It stood about ten feet tall. The back side, although rougher, felt warm where the sun's rays had shone during the afternoon hours. Emily groped for accustomed crannies and ridges to grab onto so she could haul herself up. As she did so, her hand loosened some dirt from a high spot which crumbled and fell down her neck, startling her. She stared up at the crack, then shook the debris out of her blouse, realizing that several of the crevices she'd used before must have filled with earth and sand since the last time she'd been up.

Clutching at a jagged edge, she began scaling the rock, clearing the crevices of soil as she climbed. Although it was rough going, Emily finally grasped the last ledge and heaved herself over the top. She scrambled to her feet, turned – and screamed.

Gasping in disbelief, Emily found herself facing another girl about the same age. She was so astounded she didn't say anything for several seconds, just stood with her hands over her mouth. Staring back at her was a girl dressed in an ankle-length blue print dress speckled with tiny rosebuds. Over it she wore a white apron with ruffles at the shoulder. Her sandy-coloured hair was in long braids.

"Yikes, you scared me." Emily's heart was pumping against her rib cage. "I didn't know anyone was up here." She lowered her hands to her chest as if to slow the pounding inside. "Who are you?"

"I'm Emma." The girl smiled timidly at Emily.

Emily liked the lilting sound of the girl's voice and smiled back, but wondered why she hadn't seen anyone on top of the rock as she approached. Maybe Emma had been somewhere else among the other rocks? "I never saw *you*."

"No, you were too busy climbing to notice me, lass."

"Oh." Emily was still unsure of how she'd missed seeing Emma earlier. And why did the girl talk so strangely, with the rolling r's? Why did she call her lass? Then suddenly remembering her manners, Emily introduced herself.

Emma reached for Emily's hand. "How do you do?"

Emily gave Emma's hand a limp shake in return, then drew back, wondering at the other girl's formality. And why was her hand so rough? Emily found herself staring shyly at Emma's odd appearance.

It wasn't just her long dress. The girl wore high-buttoned shoes too. She looked like one of those people who dressed up for heritage days or rodeos and exhibitions in the summer. Maybe she's just a little weird, Emily thought. Or maybe Emma isn't from around here.

"Do you live…?" Emily froze, crying out in shock as she stared over Emma's shoulder. The house and the summerfallowed field had vanished. In their place were willows and scrubby bush, thick over the open grasslands, except for the occasional stand of aspens. A creek meandered through the landscape and a huge slough lay in the distance. There were no fences. No stone piles. No elevators. Not even a gravel road — only a winding dirt trail that crawled across the plains.

"Where's my grandmother's house?" Emily felt a shudder of fear. She turned to look at Emma when the girl didn't answer right away. "Where are we?" Emily gave her head a quick shake and took another frantic look.

With a puzzled expression, Emma answered, "On top of some rocks — in the middle of the prairies. And there are no houses here. Not yet anyway."

"But my grandmother's stone house — it was right over there a few moments ago," Emily pointed at the empty knoll. "I just came from it."

Emma turned to look. "There's no house anywhere that I can see." Doubt crossed the girl's face. "We're building a sod one, but we've only started. And it's the other direction." Emma motioned behind them. "Just over there on the other side of that bluff."

Emily looked in disbelief at a ridge of trees that she'd never seen before.

"We're camping until our new house is built," Emma explained.

"When did...?"

"We've just moved to the area," said the girl, looking warily at Emily. "Where do *you* come from? I thought we were the only family in this area."

That was impossible, Emily thought. She looked wildly about her, fighting to control the panic that was making her mouth go dry. Maybe she was in the middle of a dream. Yet she could feel the wind billowing her hair, and smell the fragrance of sage and wild grass. Dreams could be vivid, but not like this.

Emma broke into her thoughts. "What's wrong, Emily? Are you lost, lass?" She touched Emily's shoulder, concern flickering in her eyes.

"I don't know. I'm not sure about anything." Emily's voice quavered, then she looked squarely into Emma's face. "I mean, one minute I'm on a rock where I've gone dozens of times with my grandmother, and I can see her house. And the next, you're here and everything I know is gone. Where are all the fences and fields?"

Looking worried, Emma suggested, "Did you maybe fall out of the back of a wagon and hit your head, lass? Maybe you've been left behind by mistake while your family has travelled on?"

"There's some kind of mistake all right, but I don't know what," Emily replied, clenching and unclenching her fists. "I've never ridden in a wagon with my family in my life. I don't know what's going on."

"Well, you must be from some place, but I've never seen anyone dressed like you. Why are you wearing such a short skirt, and with no stockings? Aren't your legs cold?"

Baffled, Emily looked at her hemline just above her knees. This encounter was getting weirder by the minute. "Well, I usually wear pants. But my mom makes me dress up for some things. It was my grandmother's funeral today."

"Oh, I'm sorry to hear about your grandmother," said Emma. Then her eyes grew wide with interest. "But you wear trousers? Only men wear trousers."

This time it was Emily's turn to look confused. "Of course I wear pants. Why are *you* dressed the way you are?" Maybe Emma was from some different kind of religious community. But that didn't explain why the landscape had changed.

"I always dress this way," Emma replied, swishing the ankle-length skirt around her legs. "This is all I have. Except my best dress for Sunday, of course."

"Of course? What do you mean – Sunday best?" Emily scraped her feet along the edge of the rock, thinking hard. She'd heard something about that kind of thing from Grandmother Renfrew. "Well…I do remember my grandmother telling me stories about when she was young," she admitted to Emma. "Something about her having only two dresses. One for everyday and one for special occasions. But that was a

long time ago when the pioneers first came and...."
Emily shivered again.

Suddenly she gasped and stared at the girl. Could it
be possible?

At the same moment Emma tilted her head,
watching Emily intently. Emily took a step backwards
near the edge of the rock and nearly lost her balance.
What on earth was going on?

CHAPTER TWO

Emily lurched forward and grabbed Emma's arm to keep herself from toppling off the rock. Stumbling ahead, she cried out in a voice shrill with panic, "I'm scared, Emma. I don't know what's happening to me. I don't know where I am."

Emma gave Emily a soothing smile. "Calm yourself, lass." She patted Emily's shoulder reassuringly. "We're in the middle of the Canadian prairies, about twenty miles south of Wolseley – at least, I think that's how far away Father said."

Emily could feel herself turn cold and clammy even though the sun was warm. The screeching of a magpie in the distance competed with her clashing thoughts. She spun around, looking at the unfamiliar landscape again, and then back at Emma.

"This can't be south of Wolseley. I mean, not the way I know it. And you – you're dressed like an early settler.

But you can't be…" Emily sputtered, her thoughts tumbling about wildly. "There's got to be an explanation."

"Well, we *are* settling here in this wilderness. And this is a new country to us," said Emma, smoothing her hands down her apron. "So I suppose that makes us settlers."

"New country? Wilderness? What do you mean?" Emily looked at the panorama of willows, water, and grasslands where tilled fields should have been. She turned again to Emma. "Where did you come from?"

"I came with my family from Scotland. First we travelled by ship across the ocean." Emma stretched out her arms. "It was so vast, and the trip…."

Emily hardly heard the last part of Emma's sentence. Her thoughts were whirring around in snippets here and there. If Emma really was from long ago and Emily had somehow slipped into the past with her…. But normal people didn't just flip into another time the way they did in some television space show, did they? She had to find an explanation.

"Okay, so you came from Scotland." Emily startled the other girl by her abrupt interruption. "But *when* did you come?"

"Well, we've been camped in this area about a month now. But it took us a long time to get here," said Emma, looking puzzled.

Emily decided to let Emma explain her situation. Maybe there'd be some clues to help them piece these strange occurrences together. She shuffled uneasily on her side of the ledge, glancing anxiously from time to time towards the spot where her grandmother's house ought to be.

In her musical voice Emma spoke of how she'd journeyed with her family from the highlands of Scotland. They'd crossed the Atlantic Ocean on a huge ship with hundreds of people squashed on board like cattle in small compartments. Allowed only a few possessions each, they'd taken the barest of necessities, a few blankets and pots and clothes in a trunk. They planned to buy whatever else they needed when they arrived.

"We were on the boat for almost two weeks. I was the only one of my family that wasn't seasick." Emma stood a little taller and tossed her braids behind her shoulders.

By now Emily was almost totally convinced Emma really was from the past, or at least that Emma herself sincerely believed she was, because of the particular way she was dressed and because she seemed so confident in relating the details of her life. And something told Emily that Emma was telling her story truthfully. Some of the details of her travels across the ocean seemed too vivid and real to be made up.

Emily listened hard as Emma explained about being on a crowded train for three days, before stopping in Winnipeg. There they'd camped for several more days in a huge tented area of the city while her father chose a homestead site from a map, and bought tools, some cows, oxen, and wagons. They'd also purchased large quantities of nonperishable food supplies. They knew they wouldn't be near a store for quite a long time, especially while they travelled.

"It took us another two weeks to get here. The weather was bad, so much snow and rain. Travelling over those rutty trails by oxcart was hard and slow."

"Oxen? Wagon?" Emily felt her knees go weak. In a barely audible voice, she asked. "What year is it according to you?"

"1899, of course."

"Wow. That's when lots of settlers started coming to Saskatchewan," said Emily, recalling her grade six studies about pioneers.

"Sask-at-chew-on?" said Emma. "What's that word? What are you saying?" She scrunched up her face. "We're in the North-West Territories."

"That proves it. This is the province of Saskatchewan. It has been since 1905." Emily stared hard at Emma. "This is just too weird. I mean, here you are back in 1899, and somehow I'm with you."

"I don't know what you mean, 'since 1905.'" Emma truly looked alarmed. "What year is it for you?"

Emily sighed shakily. "Well, just a short while ago I was at my grandmother's house after her funeral and it was 1996. Now you say it's 1899, and by the looks of everything I think you must be right. But how could that have happened?"

Emma stood silently. She seemed to be digesting what Emily had just said. Emily shifted her weight to her other foot, unconsciously twining her fingers through her hair as she gazed about the countryside. She found it incredibly hard to believe. But she was still surrounded by the same untamed prairie scene which had greeted her when she'd first met Emma on the rock.

The willow bushes along the banks of a meandering stream were more plentiful than she'd ever seen before, and there was no sign of cultivation or habitation any-where. Prairie grass blew unhindered on an empty rise where her grandmother's house had stood, and there was a single long two-track trail that stretched across the landscape instead of the crisscross of gravel roads.

"It is peculiar," said Emma, breaking the silence. "You do not seem to belong anywhere that I know of. And your clothing and speech are very different. Are you sure you have not had some accident, lass?"

"I'm positive." Emily felt more confident now that she'd begun to figure things out. The thought of trying to explain this incident to her mother even brought the briefest of smiles to her face. What would she think when Emily told her she'd gone back into the past? Emily's smile vanished as she considered her situation. How *had* she come here? Even more important, how would she get back to her own time? Would she ever see her mother or father again?

Emma shifted uncomfortably on the other side of the rock. Her face was deep in concentration.

"Now what happens? What should I do?" Emily asked out loud, in a sudden burst of concern. The hollowness in her stomach was filling with dread. She could be stuck forever in the past! Calm down, she told herself. She took several deep breaths, then carefully thought through her actions from the time she'd left her grandmother's house. There was no doubt about it, everything had been normal. Until she climbed on top of the rock and found Emma there.

Emma cleared her throat as if she was about to say something, then seemed to change her mind. She thrust her hands into her apron pockets.

"This is all so confusing," Emily said. She stood up, noticing a meadowlark flitting across the darkening sky. She must have been gone for a couple of hours. The sun was much lower on the horizon. She really had to be getting home. But how? Her parents would be worried. "How am I going to get back?"

"I'm not sure." Emma was obviously bewildered by the sequence of events. "Maybe it has something to do with the rock." She stamped her right foot down a couple of times on the hard surface. "Every time I come here I feel like something unusual is about to happen. It's always been a good feeling, though."

"Yeah, this rock is special to me, too," agreed Emily. "Maybe it has something to do with our being here together. But how do you suppose I can get home?"

Before Emma could make a suggestion, they heard a voice behind them.

"Em-ma. Em-ma. Where are you?"

Emma looked over her shoulder towards the bush several yards behind the rock.

"That's wee Geordie – my brother – come to fetch me. I'd better run. Mum will be needing help with supper and the younger ones." Emma shifted herself over the edge and down the side of the rock. Emily could hear the scraping of shoes on the hard exterior and the clatter of bits of gravel falling to the ground as Emma manoeuvred down the rock. The girl seemed anxious to be going home, and perhaps to be leaving Emily too.

A few yards beyond the rock Emily could see what looked like a narrow animal trail twisting through the scrubby poplar trees. Right at that moment a young boy in short tan pants emerged from the clump of trees. His red curly hair seemed to stick out in all directions, giving him a wild look, but a friendly lopsided grin spread across his face when he caught sight of his sister, just dropping to the ground.

"Wait!" yelled Emily, as Emma scampered down the path. "How will I get back home?"

"Try getting off the rock," Emma shouted as she ran. "If it doesn't work, come join us. Just follow the path."

Emily could hear a small voice asking Emma who she was talking to. She knew the boy hadn't seen her when she heard Emma reply, "Just the wind, Geordie." Then the voices died away.

As fast as she dared, Emily headed over to the back side of the rock. Inching to the edge, she eased herself over, feeling for footholds. It was hard to see in the quickly failing light. She felt a momentary twinge of anger at being left by herself. Emma didn't have to worry, thought Emily. She was already home. Then Emily calmed down as she realized the problem wasn't Emma's. It was hers. She just hoped she wouldn't need to find Emma's place in the dark.

She struggled to find the crevices, and her feet dangled in midair at times. From somewhere inside her head Emily could hear the echo of her own raspy breathing as she scraped along the rough surface of the rock. The rustling of her clothes seemed loud in contrast to the muted croaking of frogs somewhere in the valley.

Emily looked around in bewilderment as she descended, and shivered. It was eerie being all alone at the rock at this time of day. The air felt chilly now that the sun was sinking. She flinched at the sudden sound of water splashing in the creek nearby. What was that? Then her stomach growled, reminding her that she hadn't eaten for several hours.

Her mother was probably frantic with worry. She'd been gone so long. What if she was trapped in the past forever? Emily didn't even want to think about that possibility. But maybe she wouldn't have to. Was Emma right? Would she get back home by getting off the rock?

Emily scraped her knee on the rough surface and cried out as much from fear at her predicament as from the pain. She felt herself sliding. She knew there was a lengthy drop the last few feet to the bottom of the rock, but she'd lost track of how far she'd already descended. All at once her feet touched something firm. A great sigh of relief escaped her when she realized she'd reached the ground. She hugged the rock, afraid to leave its solidness, afraid to know what lay ahead.

Tentatively she backed away, then circled towards the face of the rock. As she stepped to the front, the sky brightened. Emily was startled to see that now the sun was only beginning to touch the horizon just beyond her grandmother's house. She whooped with delight and set off at a sprint across the meadow.

AWAY IN THE DISTANCE she could see her mother walking towards her across the yard. Relief flooded her. Then Emily realized all the vehicles were gone, except for her aunt Liz's sedan. Even her father's van was missing. She knew she was probably in deep trouble for her lengthy absence. Maybe her father was even out looking for her. She quickened her pace when she saw her mother waiting for her at the pasture gate.

"Mom, Mom," she called as she drew closer. Her breath came in ragged gulps. "I've just had the strangest experience."

Her mother appeared not to have heard her.

"I thought you were supposed to be resting. I couldn't believe my eyes when I came outside and saw you way up there by those rocks. Whatever were you doing?" Kate asked, unhooking the gate as Emily approached.

"I went for a walk to get some fresh air. It was so stuffy. I just couldn't stand it inside," said Emily, still breathing hard. "So I went up to the rock. You know, where Grandma and I always go – used to go. But then I had this bizarre thing happen."

"You're all right? You're not hurt?" Kate asked, looking Emily up and down.

Emily joined her mother on the other side of the fence. "No. I'm okay. But I want to tell you what happened when I got there. There was this girl already on the rock. Her name was Emma. But she was dressed kind of funny." Emily paused to catch her breath while she searched for the right words. "Mom, what would you say if I told you I'd just gone back into the past?"

"Oh, Emily. You and your imagination," said her mother with a heavy sigh as they started walking towards the house. "That's the wildest one yet." She stopped and turned to Emily. "You don't need to make up stories, you know. I can understand how you wanted to get out of the house. But you just should have told us you were going."

"But it's true," persisted Emily, trembling in indignation.

"Don't keep on, Emily Marie," her mother warned. "It's been a long day and I'm tired. Now come into the house. We could sure use a hand to clear the last of the lunch dishes away and get some supper started."

Offended by her mother's response, Emily stopped short and crossed her arms over her chest in silent refusal as her mother disappeared into the porch. The more she thought about it though, the more she realized how difficult it would be for her mother to understand what had just happened. Her mother didn't believe in anything she considered "fanciful," and going into the past certainly qualified in that regard.

In fact, Emily was having trouble herself coming to terms with what she'd just gone through. Now that she was safely back it didn't seem quite real somehow. Maybe her mind had been playing tricks on her. She hadn't slept well the last few nights and she was over-tired. Could she have imagined the whole thing?

Slowly she uncrossed her arms and walked into the house, opening the back door that led into the kitchen. All was quiet, except for a floor creaking and the faint muffle of voices somewhere overhead. She hadn't real-ized she'd stood outside so long.

"Mom? Mom, where are you?" Emily crossed the kitchen and yelled from the foot of the stairs. "Aunt Liz?"

Her mother poked her head out of a second floor doorway. "We'll be right down, Emily. We just have to find something. You can start supper."

Emily didn't need to be told a second time. She was hungry. Yanking open the fridge, she grabbed a casserole that one of the neighbours had brought soon after her grandmother died. She felt a pang in her chest at the reminder of her Grandmother Renfrew's death. She popped the macaroni and hamburger casserole into the oven and then plopped a wooden trivet on the oak table top. How she wished she could discuss today's strange occurrence with her Granny Renfrew.

A while later Kate and Liz appeared, dishevelled and dusty. They'd been digging in a back closet, looking for a box of special papers. As Aunt Liz sank with a sigh into a kitchen chair, she suddenly seemed old to Emily. But then she was over sixty, and she was undoubtedly exhausted after the ordeal of the last few days. As she sagged into the chair, she closed her eyes and laid her head back.

Emily's mother, too, looked tired around the eyes, but being ten years younger than Aunt Liz and the "unexpected baby" of the family, she still seemed to have plenty of energy. As Kate entered the room, she scanned the scene and deftly retrieved the casserole from the oven, plunking it into the middle of the table, while Emily finished placing the napkins by the plates.

As the three of them sat down to supper, Emily discovered that her dad had gone to drive her oldest aunt home and wouldn't return until later in the evening, and that Aunt Liz would be going to stay with some friends for the night.

Vaguely aware of the conversation going on around her, Emily forked food into her mouth and shuddered. How horrible if she'd been stuck in the past right now, instead of eating a nice hot meal with her mom and aunt. She glanced out the low kitchen window and saw the sun was just now dipping into rosy hues at the horizon. If her adventure this afternoon had been real, there must be some kind of time warp in Emma's time — like something she'd seen on *Star Trek*. Would Emma's family be eating now too? They probably didn't have many kinds of foods.

"Slow down, Emily," laughed her mother. "You'd think you hadn't eaten in days."

"Sorry, Mom. I didn't realize how hungry I was." Emily popped the last bite into her mouth and laid her fork beside her empty plate. She eyed the dessert platter across the table filled with cakes, squares, and tarts, all leftovers from the funeral. Her stomach had been too knotted up to eat much over those first few days, but she could certainly appreciate the baking now.

Aunt Liz saw her inspecting the plate of sweets and passed them to her. Emily selected a couple of brownies.

"Thanks, Aunt Liz. These are delicious."

"Agnes Barkley made them," said Kate. "She always was one of the best bakers around."

Aunt Liz wrinkled her nose and smiled. "One of the best gossips too."

"Now, Liz. Let's not start gossiping about *her*. She has a big kind heart."

"Yeah, to go with her huge body." Aunt Liz stretched her hands apart in exaggeration of Mrs. Barkley's width and laughed.

"Liz, stop that. We have to set an example for Emily." As Kate admonished her sister, her face crinkled in mirth.

Emily giggled, recalling Mrs. Barkley's portly frame. She always wore dresses with enormous flowers printed all over them. She wheezed as she walked, and snorted with loud laughter at her own raucous jokes.

Kate and Liz's talk switched to other members of the community, and Emily thought again of her afternoon with Emma. Although she'd been scared about being stuck in the past, she was curious to learn more about her experience. Had it been real? There was only one way to find out. First thing tomorrow she'd try to find Emma again.

CHAPTER THREE

Emily stretched and yawned, slowly opening her eyes. Through her open window she glimpsed patches of morning sky each time a breeze fluttered the lacy curtains. She could hear the distant cawing of crows, while nearby a robin sang from somewhere in the tall caragana hedge.

"Emily, are you awake yet?" her mother called from down below.

"I'll be right there," she shouted back. Emily knew she'd better get up soon, or her mother would come up to roust her out. And Kate would be growly if she had to climb the two flights of stairs to the attic bedroom just to hustle Emily along.

Suddenly remembering her encounter with Emma from the day before, Emily threw back the covers and hopped out of bed. Crawling onto the broad window ledge, she peered across the meadow towards the out-cropping of rocks. She couldn't see any sign of the other girl, but then realized she probably wouldn't from here. She'd have to go to the rock and somehow find a way to slip into the past again. The idea half scared, half excited her, spurring her into a frenzy of activity. Would she be able to find Emma today? Or had she just imagined everything the day before?

Emily yanked on a pair of jeans and a sweatshirt she'd left draped over the trunk at the foot of her bed. Then she raced downstairs into the kitchen where her mother was busy buttering toast.

When Emily detected only the faint lingering aroma of coffee, she knew her mother had been up for ages. Her dark hair, flecked with grey, was tied back, although little wisps had escaped, and she was wearing her "let's-get-the-job-done-right-now" sweatsuit. The kitchen was glistening and tidy.

Kate looked up and smiled as Emily slid onto a chair at the table. "My, you got down here quick this morning," she said, setting the plate of toast in front of her daughter. "Did you have a good sleep, Em?"

Emily nodded. She could hardly wait to finish eating and head outdoors. Then she decided perhaps it would be best to act casual. She knew if she seemed overanxious to leave the house her mother would become suspicious and it would take too long to explain everything. Besides, her mother wouldn't believe her story anyway.

"You certainly needed a good rest. These past couple of weeks have been tough for you, haven't they?"

A pang of sadness clutched at Emily's middle. Shifting the crumbs around on her plate with her fingers, she thought again of her grandmother's funeral the day before. Suddenly the toast seemed dry, and Emily found it hard to swallow.

"Your dad said to say good-bye. You were still sleeping when he left at six," Kate said, pouring Emily a glass of milk.

Emily washed the lumps of toast down, and nodded in response.

"This morning we have to run into Glenavon and get some boxes. We have to start packing away your grandmother's things," her mother said. "Gerald Ferguson should be here soon to pick us up."

"Aw, Mom. Do we have to do it today?" Emily couldn't believe what she was hearing. It would take ages before she could look for Emma. And wasn't her mother rushing things a little? "Couldn't we leave it for a few days? It doesn't seem right somehow going through all of Grandma's things so soon."

"The sooner the better, Em. I just want to get it over with." Kate wiped smudges off the door of the fridge. "Besides, we have to get back to the city. You have school next week and I have an advertising business to run, remember? And we'll both have a lot of catching up to do."

Emily tried another tactic. "Mom, could I stay here while you go into town?"

"Certainly not, Emily. It'll go quicker if you help." Kate picked up Emily's plate and glass and rinsed them under the tap. "Your father will be back this weekend to take us home, so we need to get as much done as we can." She began loading the dishwasher. "Your aunt Liz can only help for a couple of days. She'll be back this afternoon. The time will pass fast enough until the auction this summer."

"Auction?" Emily looked in surprise at her mother.

Kate straightened up and turned to Emily. "Yes, of course, we have to have an auction. We can't just leave everything here when we sell the place."

"What do you mean? Aren't you keeping the farm?"

"Certainly not. Who would run it?" her mother asked in surprise. "Your uncle Andrew is too old. And his sons all have farms of their own – too far away from here to make it worth their while."

Emily was stunned. She had never dreamed the farm would be sold. She knew, of course, that her parents and most of her aunts and uncles were either retired or had jobs in various cities, but how could they give up the farm where they'd grown up?

"What about Uncle Ian?" Emily blurted out with sudden inspiration. He was semi-retired, but not too old to farm.

Kate snorted. "Don't be ridiculous, Em. He's never been interested in farming in his life."

"Couldn't we just keep renting the land to Mr. Ferguson and visit here once in awhile?"

"No, Emily," her mother said in exasperation. "The decision has already been made."

"Why can't we keep the farm?" Emily whined, hating herself for doing so, but unable to stop. She knew how much it irritated her mother.

"We're selling the farm. End of discussion." Kate polished the table with vigour.

Emily stood stiffly across the room, noting that her mother wouldn't even look at her. She felt hot tears forming and quickly grabbed a tea towel off the hook by the stove to wipe her eyes. They just couldn't sell the farm! She loved it here.

Her mother's voice broke through her misery. "Let's get a move on. Gerald will be here any moment."

Just then she heard the crunch of gravel and the squeal of brakes as a vehicle slowed for the turn into their farmyard. Emily ran to wash her face, struggling to compose herself.

Plans for finding Emma had been pushed from Emily's mind completely during the last agonizing minutes of the conversation with her mother, but they returned in full force as she slammed the door after getting into Gerald Ferguson's truck. Emily stared across the pasture. She was still determined to get to the rock sometime today. If Emma was there, well and good. If not, she had plenty to think about at her favourite spot.

IN FACT, it was late afternoon before Emily managed to escape the clutches of her mother and Aunt Liz. They were forever finding something for her to do. They'd decided to start by sorting through things in the end bedroom on the second floor. Their plan was to work their way back towards the stairwell and then do the attic.

Mechanically, Emily followed their instructions, her mind elsewhere. She was trying to come to terms with everything that had been going on in her life lately. Never seeing Grandmother Renfrew again was devastating enough. Now the added blow of being unable to come to the farm once it was sold was awful. When she added the strange events of the day before to her already spinning thoughts, she felt totally overwhelmed. Somehow she managed to carry out her mother and aunt's directions.

"Put these into the hallway please, Emily." Her mother pointed to two huge garbage bags piled in one corner of the room.

Her mind still in a fog, Emily crossed the room. She groaned as she lifted the bags. "These are heavy. What's in them anyway?"

"Material scraps — for quilting."

"Quilting? All this?"

"Yes. Your grandmother never threw anything away," said Aunt Liz, with a wry smile. "She was one of the best quilters around this area too."

Emily knew this was true. Grandmother Renfrew had repeatedly won first prizes for her quilting at the country fairs in the district. Her garden produce and wild berry preserves often brought home ribbons, too.

Emily half dragged, half carried the bags through the doorway. When she returned, her mother had opened the closet door and was handing down quilts and blankets from the top shelf.

"Oh, look, Em," said her mother, unwrapping a quilt from its clear plastic bag. "Here's what's left of your grandmother's first patchwork quilt. She made it when she was ten years old."

Emily looked at it in amazement. She felt her throat tighten as she gently fingered the worn fabric. "Look at the tiny stitches – and all the different materials she used."

"These are all swatches from her family's clothing. She called it her 'crazy family quilt,'" said Aunt Liz from the other side of the room. "Considering all the relatives, I'd say that was an apt name."

Kate chuckled in agreement, refolding the coverlet gently and returning it to the bag. Emily headed towards the doorway, planning to get away.

"My goodness, I don't think Mom has had these rooms housecleaned for years," said Aunt Liz, patting her permed grey-blonde hair while surveying the mess scattered around the room.

"There's more to do than I figured," Emily's mother agreed, eyeing the stack of cartons crammed inside the closet. "I think it'll take longer than we expected to get ready for the auction."

Emily stopped short. "You're not going to get rid of all of Grandma's stuff are you?"

Her mother and Aunt Liz exchanged glances. "Well, not everything," Kate said. "We'll give some to the family. But once the farm's sold there won't be anywhere to keep most of it."

"You can't — you just can't sell Grandma's farm." Her protest came out a little louder than she expected.

"We've already been over this, Emily," Kate said quietly.

"I'm afraid we have to, sweetie," said Aunt Liz in her soft, sure voice.

Emily stood in the doorway, fighting back tears. How would she stand not being able to come and visit the farm? All the memories of her grandmother were here. As far back as she could remember, Emily had gone wandering over the land with her. She sagged against the door frame.

Through a film of tears Emily watched her mother and Aunt Liz drag a bulky box into the centre of the room. They sneezed as they wiped a layer of dust off the top.

"Be a dear, and run downstairs and bring up the dusting rag, please, Emily," her mother requested, without turning around. They opened the box and started laying old purses and scarves out on the bed. "Oh, and bring the broom and dustpan too."

Emily turned and plodded robot-fashion the length of the hallway, using her sleeves to wipe her eyes. There had to be a way to keep the farm. Clumping down the stairs, Emily could hear the two women chattering to one another. She stopped on the landing and looked out the narrow window. Brilliant sunlight flooded the meadow.

All Emily could think about was being able to spend as much time as possible out there. Somehow she had to convince her mother not to sell. She needed time to think everything through. Maybe if she hurried, they'd let her go. And maybe Emma would even be there. Although by now, Emily was having serious doubts about what she remembered of yesterday.

She ran downstairs, grabbed the cleaning tools, and scurried back up again, hoping to be excused. But her mother had other plans. Emily continued to trot up and down the stairs most of the afternoon, feeling more and more miserable.

When at last they released her, Emily's head ached and she was exhausted, but as she hurried across the greening pasture she felt a spurt of energy push her forward. The sun slanted low in the pallid sky, illuminating tiny flowers brightening among the tufts of grass. An occasional bird flitted overhead, but Emily hardly took note. She felt numb from the emotions of the day, and weary from her mother and aunt's constant commands. Regardless, she was still determined to see if she could find Emma. She scanned the rocks ahead. No sign of her, but then Emily didn't really expect to see Emma yet. Maybe she wouldn't be there. Or maybe she'd never existed.

Emily was almost out of breath by the time she scrambled up the last few feet of the incline to the huge rock. Circling around the back, she again found the familiar toeholds and ledges. She could feel the soreness in her leg muscles as she climbed. Cautiously she ascended and swung herself over the top ledge. But Emma wasn't there. And the landscape hadn't changed. She was still in the present.

She grimaced. How foolish could she be? Did she really think she'd made friends with a pioneer girl yesterday? It must have been some trick of her overtired mind. She chuckled softly to herself, but the humour of her situation quickly faded, turning to helplessness and then despair. Emily began to weep. She felt shattered, like a fragile crystal that had crashed to the floor. Everything she loved and cared for was being stripped away.

Spent at last, her body limp, Emily settled herself on her stomach overlooking the edge of the rock and scanned the coulee. She perched her chin in her hands with her elbows propped on the rock. Through puffy eyes she could see a green mist of buds veiling the branches of the willow bluff to her right. And she was sure there were more crocuses blooming than the day before. A couple of gophers ran in and out of their holes, and she thought she detected the scent of early mint in the air. She breathed deeply, and the fresh air, like a healing balm, calmed her.

As the afternoon sun warmed her back, Emily rested her head on her folded arms. In the distance she watched cotton-ball tufts of clouds floating in the pale spring-blue sky. The images shifted ever so slightly; a sleeping cat dissolved into a sailboat drifting, drifting, drifting.... Emily's eyelids felt so heavy. Perhaps she'd close them for a while. She found herself drifting too with the soft *come here and stay-a-little-while* song of the meadowlark somewhere close by.

"EMILY. EM-I-LY."

She stirred and struggled to a sitting position, squinting at the bright sunlight overhead. The sun seemed to be higher than when she'd first arrived. Through bleary eyes Emily could see Emma standing across from her on the rock. She was wearing the same long dress and white pinafore from yesterday. Emily smiled and caught her breath. "You did come! I wasn't sure if you were real yesterday."

"I couldn't get away until now," said Emma, "but I thought you might be here. And yes, I'm real." Emma looked Emily up and down, and then started giggling. "You look really funny wearing pants."

Emily grinned back at Emma. "I bet you'd probably find them more comfortable for working in. You should try them sometime." Then as Emily stretched her arms and yawned, she glanced across the valley. Gasping in surprise, she scrambled to her feet. She was in the past again.

"It's beautiful isn't it?" Emma sighed. "I love this wide open space, and the wind on my face."

Emily agreed and peered at the raw prairie below her. Now she knew she hadn't been dreaming yesterday, not unless she was having the same dream. And how incredible to be able to see the countryside as it once was, so lush and wild.

Emily fiddled with a strand of hair, twining it around a finger. Emma smoothed her wind-blown pinafore over her dress, and Emily followed her gaze over the expanse of prairie that stretched out and touched the late afternoon sky. The shrill cry of a hawk pierced the tranquillity in the shrubbery below.

"What do you see, Emma? Do you see what I see?"

"Why, that's a silly question, Emily. Tell me what you're seeing, lass. Then I'll tell you if I can see it too." Emma laughed and nudged Emily's shoulder.

"All I can see is the wind blowing the grass for miles and miles. All that wildness – nothing is like it was where I come from."

"It sounds like we are getting the same view." Emma laughed again with a musical ring.

Emily grinned back at Emma as the girl's words came out in her soft amiable voice.

Sitting down on the rock, Emily felt the twinges of soreness in her legs from all the lifting and running up and down the stairs she'd done earlier. She dangled her legs over the edge in relief, and Emma joined her. They sat in silence for a few moments, the breeze fluttering Emily's loose hair. In the distance they heard sage grouse beating their wings, calling to their mates.

"Tell me about where you come from. What's it like?" Emma asked softly.

Emily wasn't sure where to start, but she told Emma about her grandmother, the farm, and her family. Emma listened intently as Emily explained about missing almost two weeks of school since her grandmother had become sick and died. And how it was Easter break now, but soon she'd have to go back to the city.

Amazement filled Emma's face, as Emily told her of all the farms and houses everywhere. She asked the odd question here and there, and seemed amazed by Emily's explanations. Emily wasn't sure if the other girl believed her or not. Especially when Emily told Emma about her two best friends, Courtney and Samantha, and all the things they did. With a twinge of guilt Emily realized she hadn't communicated with them much for the last three weeks, had barely thought about them at all.

What were they doing back in Regina right now? Probably hanging out at the mall or over at Sam's listening to music and talking about boys. Would they believe Emily if she told them about Emma? Should she even say anything when she got back home? Maybe she'd keep Emma a secret. She'd have to think about it.

Emily glanced over at her. Emma had her eyes closed and her face raised to the sky, smiling in the sunshine. It was kind of neat having a special friend like Emma that no one knew about, even if she was a little different. The loneliness Emily had felt much of the time at the farm in the last little while was gone. "I always wanted a friend my age out here in the country, but I never thought it would be someone from a long time ago."

"You're right, it is a little strange, but I'm glad we met," replied Emma, stretching. "I'd better be getting back now. But would you like to see where I live sometime?"

"I think I would," said Emily with some reluctance. She was curious about Emma's life, but her first reaction was one of fear. What would she be getting herself into? And how would she get back to her own time again? She wasn't even sure if she could return home right now. Perhaps she'd visit Emma's family the next time they met, if there was a next time. Emily shuddered. She was more worried about seeing her own family again.

The girls climbed down the rock with Emma in the lead. As soon as she touched bottom, Emily ran to the front of the boulder. She was relieved to find that she could once again see her grandmother's farm. When she turned back to wave to Emma, the girl had disappeared, and so had the stand of poplars.

CHAPTER FOUR

Next morning Emily slipped into her jeans and a cotton sweater, and tiptoed downstairs to the kitchen, being careful to avoid the loose floorboard by the door. She propped her note near the fruit bowl on the table. In it she'd explained to her mother that she'd gone for a walk, and would be back to help in a little while.

She grabbed an apple and eased the back door open.

Streaks of dawn brightened the sky as she wiggled under the barbed-wire fence and sprinted across the pasture towards the rocky outcrop. Dandelions were beginning to show their yellow heads, and as Emily passed the willow bluff, crows cawed their greeting to the day. She quickened her pace as she neared the rock.

Emma just had to be there! She wanted to know more about her new friend. After leaving Emma last night she'd decided it was a chance of a lifetime to see an actual pioneer family in action. And especially now that the farm might be sold, there wasn't much likelihood of another opportunity.

Emily clambered up the steep incline, and scaled the rock. No Emma. Emily groaned. Not only was Emma not there; she was still looking at ploughed fields. How could she get through to Emma? Could she call to her somehow? Oh well, maybe Emma would soon appear. She could wait awhile; the sun wasn't even fully up yet.

A meadowlark sang nearby. Emily smiled at the refreshing sound. Maybe she'd climb back down and explore while she waited for Emma. Reaching the edge, she flipped on her stomach and swung her legs over. All at once she felt something grab her right ankle.

Emily squealed and looked over the edge at Emma's laughing face. "Yikes, Emma! You scared me half to death."

"That was what I had in mind, lass." The other girl giggled. "Well, you might as well keep coming down now."

"I don't know if you'll still be there if I do." Emily was remembering how Emma had disappeared the evening before when she'd moved away from the rock. She pushed her hair out of her face to get a better view of Emma there on the ground.

"Well, try. If I disappear, you can climb back up and I'll join you."

Emily slid to the ground. Emma had vanished. "Oh, no!" Emily wailed, preparing to climb back up. Then she heard giggling, and Emma's face appeared around the rock.

"Emma, that wasn't funny." Emily tried to look stern as Emma rejoined her. She'd really thought their plan hadn't worked. Then she dismissed Emma's trick with a laugh and grabbed the other girl's arm. "Come on, let's enjoy the day."

Invigorated by the slight chill that still lingered from daybreak, they ran to the front of the boulder and inspected the scene below them. A low mist rose over the meadowlands as the bright morning sun drew off the dew. A huge flock of geese flew overhead, honking loudly as they circled and settled on the broad marsh at the end of the valley.

"I feel like one of those wild birds when I'm out here," Emma said, breathing in deeply. "I wish I could stay here forever, though I've not much time today, Emily. But if you'd like to come back with me and see my family, you may."

"I'm not sure." Now that the moment had arrived for her to make a decision, Emily felt apprehensive. Deep in thought, she turned back to the rock at the same time as Emma, and they climbed on top. "I think I'd like to go, Emma. But can you tell me about your place first?"

Uppermost in Emily's mind at the moment was knowing where Emma's home was, and how long it would take to get there. What if Emily stayed too long in the past and couldn't get back? She wasn't exactly sure how any of this worked yet. It would be awful to be trapped forever. On the other hand, she was excited about seeing how Emma lived.

As Emily fidgeted, trying to make herself more comfortable, Emma explained that they had only to follow the trail a short distance through the trees and they'd come to her family's homestead. "My dad and brothers are still working on the buildings every day. We don't want to spend the winter in the tent."

"You live in a tent?" Emily was flabbergasted. She'd never imagined early pioneers living in tents. She'd only heard of sod houses or log cabins.

"What did you expect?"

"I...well, I'm not sure." Emily glanced uncertainly at Emma, mulling thoughts over in her mind. "I mean, in school we learned about pioneer families coming to settle in the west, but I didn't realize they – you – might live in a tent to start with."

"Well, there isn't anything else," said Emma, sweeping her hand across the wilderness scene before them.

"No, I guess not." Emily plucked at some imaginary fuzz on her jeans. She was trying to remember what she knew about early homesteaders and considering Emma's explanations. What was she getting herself into? Would she get back out again? Still, this might be her only chance to experience the past with her new friend.

"I've decided to go, Emma," she said decisively.

"Good. Come on." Emma led the way down the rock.

Excitement spread through Emily in waves as they dropped to the ground. She took a few steps away from the boulder. Nothing changed.

Behind Emma was the huge bluff of poplar trees with the winding trail where Geordie had come from two days ago. Masses of wispy blue harebells grew on a nearby hillside, and the sun was high in the sky.

Emma ran toward the trees. Emily stepped carefully through the clumps of grass and around stones, not sure if she should keep going. With each step, she became more confident. The surroundings remained the same.

"Wait up," she shouted. She began to run. Low branches whipped against her as she stumbled along the narrow trail. Here and there a butterfly fluttered past. She swatted at a fly that landed on her arm, conscious of the keening buzz of insects around her. It definitely was a warmer season here, Emily realized. How could that be possible? Up ahead, Emma disappeared through an opening in the trees. Emily came to a clearing and stopped.

Smoke rose from a fire in front of a grouping of three grey canvas tents and a wagon. An old woman in a long grey dress stooped over a huge pot that hung over the fire, almost like a witch tending her brew. A weird acrid smell permeated the air. What was the old woman stirring? And where had Emma gone?

Emily hung back at the edge of the bush, surveying the scene. Two massive oxen with long pointy horns chewed their cud. They were tethered to a rope fence under a stand of tall poplar trees. A few chickens were scattered about scratching the ground and clucking at their choice finds. Two pigs snorted in their log pen near the oxen, shaded from the heat of midday by another clump of trees.

The old woman wiped her hand across her brow and stood up. She looked straight at Emily. Emily felt the old lady's eyes boring right through her, yet she sensed the woman couldn't actually see her. She shivered.

Just then Emma emerged from one of the closest tents with a bundle in her arms. She waved for Emily to come over. Emily stepped forward. The woman by the fire followed Emily's progress across the clearing to Emma, but didn't speak.

"That's Granny," said Emma, when Emily tilted her head in the old lady's direction.

"She's looking at me." Emily stepped closer to Emma.

"Yes, I told Granny about you. She seems to be able to sense you, but I don't think she can see or hear you." Emma placed her hand on Emily's shoulder. "Don't be frightened."

Just then the woman nodded her head in Emily's direction. "She's here, isn't she?" she asked Emma, in a thick Scottish accent.

"Yes," Emma answered, and the old lady turned back to the huge kettle. She stooped down for another piece of wood and placed it in the fire, sending sparks and smoke into the air.

"Never mind her. Look here." Emma lifted the blanket to reveal a baby. "This is Molly. She's sweet, isn't she?"

Emily stared at two wide blue eyes staring up at her. A tiny smile lit up the baby's face as Emily leaned closer. Perhaps the infant could also sense her. "Hello there, little Molly, and how old are you?"

"Two months. She was born on the trail when we were travelling here. It's taken a fair bit out of Mother, and she needs to rest a great deal. Especially with this hot sun." Emma eased the baby over her shoulder and patted her tiny back. "I help with Molly whenever I'm free from working in the garden or making meals."

Emily shifted her feet, unsure of what to do next. The strange smell coming from the pot over the fire burned in her nostrils. And the warmth of the sun made her itchy wherever her sweater touched her skin. She wished she hadn't worn it. But how could she have known it would be more like summer here? Scratching at her back, she watched Emma make faces at Molly. The baby gurgled and waved her arms in the air.

Behind the tents Emily could see an enormous patch of raw earth where the low grassy clearing had been cut out and dug down about a foot. Just at that moment Geordie emerged from around a bush, pushing a crude handmade wooden wheelbarrow. He rumbled it over to the woman by the fire, not seeming to notice Emily at all. Together the woman and boy lifted the huge pot and poured the slimy white contents into the mud-caked wheelbarrow. Geordie hoisted the weathered handles up and set off in the direction from which he'd come. The wheel ground into the track, and Emily could see he was struggling to keep the barrow from tipping over. "What on earth is he doing?"

"Hauling a mixture of lime and clay to fill in the cracks of the sod house, so the wind won't blow through come winter." Emma untangled the baby's fingers from her hair.

"Where's the house?" Emily craned her neck, looking.

Emma pointed over her shoulder. "Just over that knoll. Come on, I'll show you. Just let me give Molly back to Mother, so she can feed her." Emma darted back into the tent as the baby began to whimper.

They walked through the open grassland and over the swell of prairie, following a trail packed hard by the travel of many feet. Emily swished bluebottle flies off her arm and scurried along. Just over a ridge the path suddenly opened onto a brilliant carpet of red lilies.

"Prairie lilies," Emily squealed with delight. She jerked to a stop. "I've never seen so many in my life. We hardly ever see them any more."

"Oh, is that what they are? They're beautiful, aren't they?"

Both girls stopped and breathed deeply. Then laughed. They could only smell the wild clover and primroses at the edge of the meadow.

"Wait a minute. They're not supposed to bloom until mid-June." Emily shook her head.

"It is June. June 18, to be exact."

Emily stared, open-mouthed. "But it's April. I only came to the rock yesterday." That explained why it was so hot here. She grabbed Emma's arm. "Not only have I gone back in time, but it's speeding up as well. I wonder what's happening back at home? Maybe I should go."

"Take a quick peek at the building, then we'll run back." Emma started forward, trying to drag Emily with her.

Emily drew back. What if everything had changed back home and she'd actually been gone for several months? Would her parents have given up looking for her by now? Maybe they'd returned to Regina and she'd find no one back at the house. Of course, if no one was there, it wouldn't matter if she was a few minutes later than she was already. Emily turned and ran to catch up to Emma.

Just then they stepped over another hillock and Emily forgot for the moment that she was in a hurry. Three bearded men, dressed in overalls and grey shirts with the sleeves rolled up, were hauling huge squares of sod off a wagon and stacking them up like bricks to form the four walls of a building. Two oxen were tied to the wagon, snorting and swishing their tails at the flies. Nearby another sod structure was already complete and two teenaged girls were scooping the white mixture from Geordie's wheelbarrow with huge paddles and patting it onto the walls.

"There's our house. Isn't it grand?" asked Emma. "Now we'll be snug for the winter."

Emily looked at the girl in disbelief. Snug for the winter? How could Emma think that? The place was little more than a low shack, made of mud and grass. It had no glass windows, only slatted shutters. True, the walls were thick, but the roof was only logs with more sod on top.

"How will you heat it?" Emily asked, amazed that anyone could exist in that kind of house during a cold prairie winter.

"With wood, of course." Emma seemed unconcerned and pointed to the other structure going up. "That's the shed for the animals."

An instant later Geordie appeared with an armload of dry wood from the nearby stand of aspens and added it to the huge stack between the two buildings. Obviously this was their wood supply for the winter, Emily realized.

On the other side of the wood pile, two smaller girls chased each other through the long grass, yelling as they went. In the distance Emily could see a small field with green shoots waving in the wind. Beyond it the red stems of willow were mirrored in a glassy slough rimmed with marsh marigolds.

An older girl, with long dark hair braided and piled on top of her head, was hoeing in a garden several yards from the house. "Emma. There you are, lass. Were you gadding about?" The girl swept some loose strands of hair from her forehead and leaned on her hoe, totally unaware of Emily's presence. "Come help me with the gardening if you're not looking after Molly."

"I can't right now, Bella. I told mother I'd be right back," Emma called, and then turned to Emily. "Let's get you home."

The two girls raced back through the campsite, dashed down the trail through the trees, and climbed onto the rock.

"That was really great," Emily panted as she collapsed onto the top of the slab and lay on her back.

"I'm glad you came," Emma gasped, joining Emily on the flat surface. They stared up at the hazy afternoon sky, trying to catch their breaths.

"Wouldn't it be wonderful if I could come and visit you anytime – even without you having to be with me?" Emily was already thinking of going back again.

"I think I may know a way." Emma sat up. "Here, I've brought you something." Out of her apron pocket, she pulled a small embroidered pouch with leather thongs and thrust it toward Emily.

"What is it?" The bag was heavy and felt lumpy.

Emma loosened the opening. Emily peered inside. "Stones?" she said.

"Special stones. From Scotland. I brought some of my homeland with me – in case I never go there again. Go on, pick one."

Emily drew a large dark stone out of the pouch. It felt cool and smooth in her sweaty hand. "What's it for?"

Emma explained how she'd told her grandmother all about Emily. Although the older woman had been mystified and fearful at first, she believed such things could happen and was curious. "Gran reckoned if I gave you something of mine you'd be able to enter more easily and maybe even stay without me." She ran over to the edge of the rock. "Come on. Let's see what happens."

Clutching the stone tightly, Emily clambered down behind Emma. They reassured each other that if it didn't work they'd meet back on top.

"Very well now, put the stone down," Emma said when they reached the bottom. "And I'll leave." She ran towards the trees.

Reluctantly Emily placed the stone on the ground. As she withdrew her hand she felt a tremor run through her body, and she was back in her own time. At least she thought it was the same season as when she'd left. She could see leaves budding out on the trees, so it must still be April. And there was no Emma. Quickly she snatched up the small stone again. Emma reappeared by the stand of trees.

"It worked!" Emily gasped. She stared at the rock in her open hand.

"It worked," Emma yelled, returning to Emily's side.

"But now what?" asked Emily, holding the stone firmly in her grasp. She knew Emma was about to leave for real this time. "What do we do with the stone? If you take it, I'll have to wait for you each time I want to go into the past. And if I hang on to the stone I'll always be in your time."

"How about if we leave it here somewhere safe? Then you could come and go as you please," suggested Emma.

"Great idea, but where could we hide it?" Emily scanned the rock. "Maybe in one of those crevices."

The girls examined them. One of the toeholds was deeper than the others and slanted inwards.

"No one will find it here." Emily looked at Emma for reassurance.

"Good. I have to go. See you soon." She gave Emily a quick wave and ran towards the bush.

As soon as Emily could no longer see Emma, she set the stone in the crevice. She shuddered, and the trees where Emma had run vanished.

Emily dashed for home. She ran harder when she saw how high the sun was in the sky. She hoped this was the same day that she'd left. Her mom was going to be furious. She'd been gone longer than she'd expected.

CHAPTER FIVE

Emily didn't notice the dark clouds gathering in the west as she reached the farmyard. But out of the corner of her eye she saw Gerald Ferguson, hurrying from the tractor to his truck, by the granaries at the bottom of the nearby field. She slackened her pace, concentrating on what excuses she'd give for being gone all this time. If only she knew exactly how long she'd been away from the house, it would help. Her mother could be a real bear sometimes, and there was no telling how she'd react this time. Perhaps the straightforward approach would work best.

She let the porch door bang open and stepped into the quiet kitchen. Her earlier note was gone. Cereal bowls and coffee mugs were drying on the drainboard near the sink. Oops, she'd missed breakfast, but at least it seemed to be the same day that she'd left, according to the calendar. It was turned to the right date. Emily glanced at the clock above the wainscotted wall. Eleven-forty. Almost lunch time. Her stomach gurgled in agreement. She sprinted up the stairs and yelled.

"Mom? Aunt Liz? I'm back. Sorry I took so long."

There was no answer.

"Mom?"

She walked along the hallway, peering into each of the four bedroom doorways as she went. She was met with silence. Then she heard a scraping sound along the floor above her. They must be in the attic. She opened the door and hollered again as she ascended the narrow staircase.

"Hello. I'm back."

"It's about time, young lady," said her mother. "Your aunt Liz and I could sure use a hand. There's a lot of work to be done."

Emily poked her head up through the opening. Her mother and aunt were working in one half of the attic. Two rooms were separated in the attic by a slatted wall. The one side had later been plastered and painted to create the bedroom which Emily used; the other was for storage.

The two women were bending over a trunk. In one corner were shapes on the dust-covered floor where boxes and old pieces of furniture had stood. The objects themselves were spread along one wall. Corners of wallpaper were curled and discoloured with mildew. The whole place smelled of dust and dead air, so different from the refreshing environment Emily had just left.

"It was such a fantastic morning. You should have come out. You can't stay inside all the time," Emily said, wrinkling her nose in disgust.

She shuffled near the window at the low-ceilinged end of the room as the two older women continued to work. She was surprised to see the yard lit by an unusually bright sun. Dark banks of clouds were forming over the barn, and the leaves of the poplar trees twirled in sudden gusts of wind. A storm was about to break.

"There's more to life than gadding about, young lady."

Emily gazed at her mother's back, realizing she had used the same term – "gadding about" – as Emma's sister had done.

Kate flipped open a box with a bang, making Emily jump. Aunt Liz, with exaggerated calm, handed Emily's mother a stack of old hats from the trunk to place inside it.

"More to life?" Emily placed her hands on her hips, responding to her mother's remark. "Like what, Mom? More work? You're always working. Why don't you take a break and go for a walk sometime?" Emily snapped, just as a low rumble of thunder sounded in the distance.

"There's so much to do. You know that." Kate looked at Emily in exasperation.

"You always say that. Even at home. It doesn't matter how much I help you. There's always more to do."

"That's enough, Emily. Don't talk to me like that." Her mother shook an old handbag at her. "Go down and make some sandwiches, young lady. Liz and I have been working hard all morning, and we're hungry."

Emily ducked her head and stamped down the stairs in silence. She'd had such a lovely morning. Why did her mother have to ruin it? Just then a flash of lightning lit up the stairwell. Emily looked out the landing window as she passed. Droplets of rain struck the panes. Storm clouds were quickly obscuring the sun.

What about soup? Maybe if she put a little extra effort into lunch and made some hot vegetable soup to go with the sandwiches, her mom would thaw a little. Emily sighed, opening the cupboard door. This might be a long day.

THEY WERE FINISHING LUNCH when the phone rang. Emily reached it first.

"Hi, Dad. Yeah, it's raining here too." Emily listened for awhile. "Oh. All right. I'll get Mom." She handed the receiver to Kate, whispering loudly to Aunt Liz as she regained her chair at the table, "It's Dad. He can't come and pick us up this weekend."

"Oh, that's too bad," said Aunt Liz. "I have to leave in the morning too. I won't be able to get down for another couple of weeks. There's so much to do before the auction."

Emily grimaced at the word auction. She still hadn't figured out how to persuade her mom and aunt not to sell the farm.

Kate tugged at the sweatband holding her hair back from her face as she walked back to the table. She had a scowl on her face. "Great – David has some big unexpected meeting in Victoria with some geologists from Mexico. And I have to get back in to work. Lindsay is having a fit trying to manage the business without me. We have too many deadlines. I don't know what to do."

Liz crunched on a carrot stick, a concentrated look on her face. "There's nothing we can do. We'll just have to hold the auction later in the summer."

"That goes without saying," Kate looked with disgust at her sister. "I mean, how will we get back to Regina?"

"Don't look at me." Liz held up her hands as if warding off the inevitable. "You know I'm heading to Winnipeg. And no, I won't make a detour. You know how I hate driving on the highway any more than I have to."

"Darn that old car of ours. Why did it have to break down last week? I don't want to take the bus. We've too much to take back with us."

Emily was hardly aware of Kate stacking plates and carrying them to the dishwasher. Her mind was reeling. The auction might be delayed. She still might have time to think of something to stop it altogether. This old house and the farm where she'd spent so many happy hours meant so much to her. Why couldn't she make her mother see how important it was to keep it? This place was all she had left of her Grandmother Renfrew.

Emily, watching her mother scrape off the plates before placing them in the dishwasher, suddenly pictured her grandmother bustling about the kitchen. She recalled how the elderly lady had insisted on modernizing everything in it. "All these gadgets speed up the work so I have more time to enjoy the outdoors," she'd said, winking at Emily. Emily smiled, remembering their private understanding.

"What are you grinning at?" Kate's irritated voice broke into her thoughts.

"Just something I saw on TV." Emily rose from the table and quickly began putting food in the refrigerator. And then the rain began pelting the kitchen window, and Emily could hardly see the barn across the yard.

"By the way, Emily, what were you doing all morning?"

"I — I visited with that girl I told you about the other day. Remember?" Emily's mind raced over possible explanations. She didn't want to risk getting into another argument with her mother.

"You mean there really was someone up on those rocks?"

"Yes. The same girl." Emily ducked her head back into the fridge, hoping to avoid more questions.

"I thought you were just telling me another one of your stories. So what was she doing there? And don't try to embellish like you did last time." Kate shook a finger in warning.

"Uh, well, uh…." Emily didn't know how to answer the question. If she told her mother the truth, she'd never believe her. In fact, she'd probably think Emily was ready for the loony bin. Then again maybe the truth would work. At least part of it.

"Well? What did you learn about her? Where's she really from?"

"Emma. That's her name. She came with her family from Scotland." So far so good.

"Really? And whose place did they buy?" Kate thought for a moment. "Maybe they bought the old McGuillivray place. I think I heard something about it changing hands."

"I'm not sure who owned it before." True enough, Emily didn't know whose land it was. She wasn't sure where the boundary of her grandparents' half section fell. "They're building a new house. They're camped out right now – until it's finished."

Emily decided she'd better not elaborate any more, and headed for the bathroom to hide out for awhile.

"What did you say her last name was?" Her mother called after her.

"I don't know. I forgot to ask." Emily took the stairs two at a time, smiling wryly to herself. She really had forgotten to ask Emma her last name. She'd have to remember to question her tomorrow. Right now she wanted to scribble down the few things she did know about Emma.

Emily was still writing when Kate and Liz came back upstairs. They knocked on the opposite side of the adjoining wall, inviting Emily to come and help.

"All right," she called. With a sigh she snapped her notebook closed and stashed it under the window ledge. There was just enough room to place something between the wall and the ledge. Emily had used the hiding place for as long as she could remember. No one else knew about it. Then she heard more knocks on the wall.

"Coming."

Opening her door, Emily stepped down two steps and around the wall and back up again to where her aunt and mother were already sorting through the trunk. She noticed the pattering of the rain was louder over here, and the room seemed dark and gloomy. Even though several lights and lamps were turned on, they didn't illuminate the far-reaching corners of the attic. The place was damp and cool. Emily was glad she had worn a sweater.

She sauntered over to one of the boxes and pulled open the lid. More boxes inside. Shoeboxes, card boxes. She pulled one out and sat on the edge of the windowsill. Stacks of yellowed newspaper clippings taken from the *Family Herald* filled the box; recipes her grandmother had saved, intending to paste into a scrapbook. Emily conjured up the smell of the flour and water glue her grandmother mixed to do that sort of job.

In fact, somewhere around this house, Emily had a couple of scrapbooks that she'd pasted her own clippings into when she was much younger. She'd trimmed nice pictures of flowers, horses, and cuddly baby animals from the *Western Producer* and *Country Guide*. That was a pastime her grandmother had suggested on rainy days. Days like today.

"Look at these old clothes," Aunt Liz exclaimed from the other side of the attic. She held up a floor-length blue taffeta gown that she'd extracted from another trunk.

Emily and Kate joined her in sorting through the garments. Emily spied a white hat covered with blue ribbons and lace. She perched it on her head. "Hey, it matches that dress you pulled out, Aunt Liz."

Holding the wide-brimmed hat on her head with one hand, she sifted through the clothing and pulled out the gown with the other. A few minutes later Emily stood in the entire outfit, sneezing. The dress fit as if it had been made for her.

"Whew, this smells musty. It must have been packed away for ages." The gown, which reached Emily's ankles, rustled as she moved about, making her feel like she'd stepped into Emma's time again. Emily removed it with care and laid it back into the trunk.

Her mother and aunt watched her try on several other outfits, each more intriguing than the previous one. The bathing suit that almost covered the whole body set all three to laughing. Then Aunt Liz found an old umbrella. She opened it over Emily's head with a flaring gesture that sent them into gales of laughter when they discovered it was so full of holes that it was useless. The sound of the wind increasing and the rain pushing down harder, made them laugh all the more, as Aunt Liz waved the umbrella about in a pantomime of trying to keep dry.

Kate tucked the garments back into the trunk to the accompaniment of their fading laughter. Emily yawned. The monotonous sound of the rain thrumming on the roof just above their heads made her sleepy. She peered out through the window at the pelting rain washing down the glass. The wind rattled the panes.

What was Emma doing right now? Was it raining there? How did they manage if it was? Maybe they'd finished their house and were already living in it. She set the box of recipes on the floor and reached for another, finding more of the same. Box after box, Emily opened and peeked inside. Why on earth had her grandmother even saved these recipes? She had always cooked from memory. Emily had never seen her grandmother follow directions for making anything.

Only one big box remained at the bottom. Emily reached in and lifted it out. It seemed heavier than the others. She pried off the lid. Photographs, and some-thing underneath. She shuffled through the pictures. Nameless people stared back at her from the backs of binders and threshers and from inside buckboards. Some stood beside old Model T's or held reins of oxen ploughing a field. Emily found a huge wedding group photograph with twenty or thirty people posed in it.

"Wow. Everyone really got into the wedding pictures years ago. Look at this, Mom." She handed Kate the photo. "Do you know who the bride and groom are?"

"No, just some relatives." She handed it back to Emily, then grabbed it back again. "Wait now. That could be your great-uncle Alex's wedding to Aunt Sue. He was your grandma's oldest brother. Or was it one of the others we never knew? I forget." She flipped the photo over. "Yes, it says right here – Alexander and Susannah Elliott, 1900."

"That's a long time ago."

"Sure is. Didn't they take wonderful photos back then?" The picture Kate held was on stiff card, torn at one corner and faded yellow with time, but the images were sharp and clear.

"What are these?" asked Emily, staring down at a stack of dark squares of glass on the bottom of the box.

Kate looked inside. "Oh, the glass negatives!" Delight spread across her face. "So, that's where they got to. I always wondered."

"Glass negatives?" Emily looked puzzled. That explained why the box was so heavy, but she didn't understand what they were.

"Yes. People used to develop their own pictures even in the 'olden days,'" Liz explained, ruffling Emily's hair.

"How did it work?" asked Emily, turning over one of the square plates in her hands.

"Well, you see how one side is just plain glass and the other side has a thin layer of something that's kind of chipping off there on that corner? Well, that's the emulsion," explained Aunt Liz, getting excited about the subject. "They painted this chemical on the pieces of glass in the dark. Then exposed them in the camera and developed them."

"Their darkrooms weren't fancy. They were really just a few trays of developing chemicals on a dresser in the bedroom," Kate interjected. "They just used a flashlight with a red cloth over it as a light to work by."

"Your grandmother had her own darkroom too, you know," Aunt Liz added.

"She did?" asked Emily.

"Sure, her old camera and developing equipment must still be around here some place."

"Neat," said Emily. "I want to see them when you find them. Can we look at these? They look kind of fragile."

"Sure," said Kate, moving closer to Emily. "We just have to be careful with the edges. They're a little rough."

"I bet some of these are ones your grandmother took," said Aunt Liz.

Emily handed her mother the box and Liz joined them as they sat down on the floor. Sitting together in the tight circle made Emily feel safe and warm, and she was able to ignore the darkness of the thunderstorm outside.

"Let's see if they match up with the photos," Liz suggested. They cheered each time they found a photograph and negative that corresponded. Only two negatives weren't reproduced.

"This one is your grandma and grandpa's wedding photo. I know there's a copy of it in one of the photo albums downstairs somewhere," said Liz, handing the negative to Emily.

"Can I see the photo?" asked Emily.

"Sure, whenever I come across the albums, I'll dig it out for you."

"I've never seen this one before." Kate held the piece of dark glass towards the light bulb, squinting at it. "It looks like a family group, an older couple with eight kids, maybe."

"Let me see." Emily peered over her mother's shoulder. Just then the light flickered, and an instant later a crash of thunder boomed overhead. Kate put her arm around Emily, drawing her closer as they examined the negative together.

"I think that's maybe your greatgrandparents when they first came out west," said Liz. "Could be some other family though. I don't really recognize anyone, but it's hard to tell from a negative."

"Wow, what a big family," said Emily. "When would they have come?"

"Sometime in the 1890s, I think," replied Liz.

"Wow, just like Em —" Emily stopped short. She'd almost said "just like Emma and her family." Her mother and aunt didn't seem to notice the slip. Emily wondered if Emma would have known their ancestors. She'd go and ask her. Or maybe she could show her the picture. She could hear the steady drumming of the rain on the roof, and knew she wouldn't be going anywhere for awhile.

"Could we get a print made of it?" Emily blurted out.

"I suppose so," said Kate. She noted the pleading look on Emily's face. "I could probably get Dwayne to print one for us in the darkroom over at the newspaper office."

"I wouldn't mind one of Grandma and Grandpa's wedding either. Could you get one made for me too, Mom?"

"Me too," said Liz, laughing.

"I might as well make one for the rest of the family while I'm at it," said Kate, chuckling. She patted Emily's shoulder. "I'll see if I can get Gerald Ferguson to take us tomorrow."

"Great," said Emily. She stood up and started across the attic. She could hardly wait to ask Emma if she'd known her family.

"Wait a minute, young lady. You're not going to leave a mess like this, are you?" Kate swept her arm over the photos spread on the floor.

"Uh, no, I guess not. Maybe I should put these negatives in a safe place."

"Good idea."

Emily found a small box and tucked the negatives in, separating them with tissue paper she found. "I'll just put these in my room."

"Okay, but come right back."

Emily hurried to her bedroom and slid the box under the ledge of the window seat as thunder rumbled farther in the distance. The rain was gushing down in torrents, the wind whipping the trees outside. The dark leaden sky did not show any signs of clearing. She knew there was no chance of going out again today. But first thing tomorrow she'd look for Emma once more.

CHAPTER SIX

The next morning Emily awoke to the squawk of sparrows when Aunt Liz opened her bedroom window. The air smelled fresh and clean in the aftermath of yesterday's rain.

"Wake up, sleepyhead." Aunt Liz laughed and jostled Emily's arm as she sat down on the edge of the bed. "I have to leave, Em. Gotta get back to Winnipeg."

"Bye, Aunt Liz. I'll see you in a couple of weeks." Emily sat up sleepily and gave her aunt a hug. "Have a safe trip back."

"Thanks, kiddo. Take care of yourself." Her aunt got up and went across the room towards the door, then paused at the head of the stairs. "By the way, Emily. I had a talk with your mother last night about taking it easier, not working so hard. She said she'd try, but you know how she is."

"Yeah, I know. She's a workaholic." Emily fiddled with her hair, and lay back on the pillow. "I just wish she'd take time to go out for a walk or a bike ride or something. She never relaxes."

"She's under a lot of pressure, you know. Trying to meet demands and pay the bills. It's not easy running your own business. But it's important that she take time for herself too." Liz walked over to the mirror and straightened her blazer. Emily liked the way her aunt dressed — a professional, yet casual look, not too old-ladyish. Her grey-blonde hair was neatly in place, yet it looked natural. Aunt Liz smoothed her skirt and headed for the stairs again. "I'll work on her when I get back. In the meantime, just keep inviting her for walks and maybe she'll take you up on it sometime."

"Okay, Aunt Liz. Thanks."

"Bye, sweetie."

"Bye."

Aunt Liz's head disappeared down the staircase and Emily slid out of bed. As she dressed she could see her aunt get into her car and drive off, showering gravel down the driveway as the car sprinted away. Someday I'm going to have a car just like that, thought Emily. Then she dashed down the stairs, meeting her mother in the second floor hallway.

"Morning, Mom. Could I go see if I can find Emma…?" She stopped short. She'd almost blurted out "and ask her about her family?" Good thing she'd caught herself before her mother asked more awkward questions.

"Morning, Em. Well, I guess so." Kate's face creased with a frown, as she considered Emily's request. "I have to spend some time with Gerald Ferguson going over the business arrangements for the farm this morning. But this afternoon you'll have to come with me to town — if I can get Gerald to give us a ride." Kate looked at her daughter and suddenly gave her a hug. "You go on, but grab something to eat first, okay?"

"Okay. Thanks, Mom." Emily was relieved. She and her mom had a truce again. She raced downstairs.

In the kitchen Emily scrounged around for a plastic bag, then grabbed a sandwich left over from lunch the day before and tucked it inside. Outside, Mr. Ferguson, who was just driving into the yard in his half-ton, waved and grinned at Emily. He was knocking on the door as she strolled across the prairie, chewing her egg-salad sandwich.

The ground was damp. She could feel the moisture leaking into her sneakers. Wet grass and weeds smacked at her pant legs, until the bottoms were soaked to her calves, but she didn't care. The foliage everywhere was brilliant green, and the sun glinted off the bright blue of the slough as she passed. Two swallows swung and dipped over the power lines, headed for her grandparents' barn. The leaves on the trees had seemingly popped out fully from buds overnight, and the air smelled fresh and clean.

Emily breathed deeply and ran. When she reached the boulder she climbed part way up and groped in the crevice for the special stone. She'd decided to take it with her in case Emma hadn't come. Just as she touched its smooth coolness, she trembled and felt herself slipping…The scenery shifted. She slid the stone into the pocket of her jeans, then scaled the top of the rock – where Emma waited for her.

"Hi, Emma. Isn't it a glorious day?"

"Indeed, it is a grand July day, Emily." Emma rose to greet her. "Come on, lass. I want to show you our new home. We moved in a couple of weeks ago."

The two girls climbed down from the rock and followed the trail across the meadow.

"It poured buckets yesterday," Emily exclaimed as they waded through vegetation dripping with moisture. "Looks like it did here, too."

"Yes, it rained here, but we were cosy and dry in our new house." Emma stopped and bent over. Her fingers parted the foliage. "Look Emily. Mushrooms."

"Don't touch that, Emma. That one's poisonous. I can show you some good ones to eat, though. Grandmother Renfrew taught me how to hunt for mushrooms. You have to be really careful which ones you pick, but there should be lots of good ones after this rain."

Emily scampered through the grass and found what she was looking for. "Look, Emma, these ones are okay, but not those over there." Emily pointed to individual mushrooms scattered here and there. "Don't touch those. They're really deadly. My grandma said you should always pick mushrooms with someone who knows what they're doing," Emily warned her friend.

She showed Emma the band of good mushrooms, and both girls were soon spotting them all over the meadow. They picked the spongy morsels, but soon had too many to hold in their hands. The mushrooms were too dirty to wrap in Emma's apron. That was when Emily remembered the plastic bread bag from her sandwich. She pulled it out of her pocket.

Gazing in amazement at the clear bag, Emma reached out and rubbed the pliable material in her fingers. "Oooh, what is this?" she squealed, making a disgusted face. Setting the mushrooms on the ground, she held the bag up to her eyes and peered at Emily through it.

While Emma tested the bag with her fingers, Emily tried to explain about plastic and its uses. By the time she was done, both girls were giggling at the distortion the plastic created as they peered through it. When their laughter subsided, they popped the mushrooms into the bag and resumed picking.

As they worked, Emma explained that they had baskets for carrying things and sometimes they used cloth or leather sacks. Soon the girls were discussing the differences between modern inventions and items used in the past. Emma was amazed to hear about television and disc players, and Emily laughed when Emma described having to hand crank a phonograph to hear music recorded on grooved cylinders.

Their talk eventually brought them back to a discussion about wild plants and mushrooms. Emily told Emma how she and her grandmother had harvested mushrooms around the edges of the manure pile after a rain. She told Emma how the little buttons appeared as if by magic overnight and how good they tasted fried fresh in butter with toast. If they were plentiful her grandmother also canned them, but that meant many hours of gathering.

"Sometimes," she said, standing up and stretching her aching back, "we'd cross the whole meadow and pick them." Emily sighed, remembering Grandmother Renfrew and their outings together. Oh, how she missed her favourite person.

Squatting on the ground again, Emily glanced down at her sodden runners and realized her feet were thoroughly wet. She should have worn rubber boots. She started giggling again, then tried to explain to Emma how she and her grandmother clomped about in rubber boots after a rain. As Emily demonstrated, both girls burst into fits of laughter, startling a gopher that had poked his head out of a nearby hole.

The girls continued collecting mushrooms until Emily's bag was full, stopping only occasionally to swat at mosquitoes and dodge the grasshoppers vaulting about them. Or to stand and stretch in the heat of the strong summer sun.

"This is wonderful, Emily. I'll take these to Granny and we'll have something different to eat with our stewed rabbit tonight." Emma held the bag up high and giggled again.

Emily smiled wanly at the thought of eating a poor defenceless wild rabbit. When she considered the options though, she realized there wasn't a great deal of choice. Emma's family certainly couldn't go to a grocery store and stock up on supplies.

"What else do you eat, Emma?" asked Emily, curious now.

"Porridge, every morning, for sure. And oat-cakes or bread. Sometimes wild fowl. You know – ducks, geese, grouse. Once in a while either my father or one of my brothers shoots a deer."

Emily paled again at the thought of a deer, but realized that even in the 1990s, people hunted them for sport and food.

"We've found some wonderful berries to eat too," Emma added. "Raspberries, and some purplish-black ones like blueberries, although they're not quite the same as the ones we grew back home. They're plentiful right now."

"Can you show me where they are?"

"Sure."

Both girls ran to the edge of the woods where some bushes hung low to the ground, pulled down by the weight of ripe purple berries.

"Saskatoons! My favourite." Emily grabbed a handful and popped them into her mouth. The sharp taste of the juicy fruit reminded her instantly of picking berries with Grandmother Renfrew.

Every summer her grandmother had made pies, canned dozens of jars of preserves, and frozen huge quantities to be used over the winter months. The best were fresh berries, heaped with sugar, swimming in fresh farm cream.

Emily felt numb for a moment when she realized her grandmother would never do these things again. In fact, Emily might never do them again either, if the farm really sold. So far she hadn't been able to come up with a way to convince her family to keep it. Shrugging off the feeling of depression, she hurried after Emma, who had gone around to another side of the bush.

Both girls ate berries until they were full, laughing at their purple-stained tongues and fingers. Then they wandered along the edge of the bluff, where a profusion of wild raspberries grew. They had a handful each, but were too stuffed to eat more. Besides, the mosquitoes were attacking the girls in larger numbers, and they were tired.

"I'll tell my granny and we'll come out and pick these later too."

"What about your mother?" asked Emily. "How is she?"

"Poorly. She's not regaining her strength like she should. She's worried, but we are all doing what we can to help."

"I'm sorry to hear she's sick." Emily thought for a few moments. "You know, I remember my grandmother used to say camomile tea was good for almost any kind of ailment. Has your mother tried it?"

"I've heard of it back in Scotland, but I didn't know it grew here too."

"Sure – it grows wild all over the pasture." Emily pointed to a plant with her wet sneaker. "It's just starting to bloom. See? You can pick it and steep it like tea. It can be dried, too."

"Well, aren't you wonderful, Emily."

Emily grinned. "The thanks go to my grandmother. She knew everything about plants and I just listened. She said camomile was great for curing almost anything."

"Come on, lass. Let's take this to my home and then we'll come back with a basket for some of this camomile," said Emma. She snatched up the bag of mushrooms from the ground where they'd left it and headed into the trees.

The girls hurried up the path and across the clearing to the new building site. Huge clusters of mosquitoes hovered above their heads, causing the girls to flail their arms in the air as they ran. Once they reached the buildings, Emily discovered a huge smouldering fire in the yard, from which billowed clouds of smoke that seemed to be keeping the mosquitoes at bay. All the livestock were pressed against their compound fences, huddling as close as they could to the smudge for relief from the biting pests.

Emily was amazed to find the sod buildings finished. Emma drew her inside the compact house, where she stepped onto a packed dirt floor. Although the interior was dark and damp with thick walls, Emily felt the cosiness of Emma's new home. The single room was neatly furnished with a wood cookstove, a solitary table, a couple of benches, and a few chairs. A quilt hung across the middle of the room, concealing several cots and beds made up on straw mats on the floor.

The baby, Molly, was asleep in a cradle with netting stretched over the opening, and her mother lay on a bed beside her, looking pale and worn. Emma quietly crossed to a cupboard on the far wall and dumped the mushrooms into a bowl. Then she covered them with a cloth, and tiptoed back out into the sweltering heat of the day with Emily close behind her.

"Mother needs her rest. She's been up since early morning doing the laundry," Emma explained as she wadded up the plastic bag and handed it back to Emily.

Emily tucked it into her pants pocket. "Guess you'd have a hard time explaining this, wouldn't you?"

Emma grinned. "Come on, I'll show you the garden."

Emily couldn't believe her eyes at the size of the plants, but when she thought about it, she realized over a month had passed in Emma's time. Bella was in the garden again, this time directing the younger children on how to pull weeds. She waved at Emma and asked her to bring a bucket of water to the thirsty crew.

Emily followed Emma through a stand of poplars, where they found a wooden pail turned upside down over a plank lid. The handle of the pail was tied to a rope. Emma heaved the solid lid up and threw it aside with a thunk, then dropped the bucket into the deep dark hole. Emily could hear the splash when it hit water. Emma jerked the rope until the pail sank, struggled to pull the heavy load back up again, then grabbed a dipper hanging on a nearby tree. As she hauled the bucket back to the garden, the water sloshed onto her feet and the hem of her dress, but she didn't seem to mind.

"Tell me who everyone is," Emily asked, as they walked along.

"All right," said Emma. "You already know Bella — Isabella, really. She's 17 — my oldest sister. The younger ones are Elsbeth — Beth for short, she's named after my mother, and Katherine, although we call her Kate. She's the serious one of the bunch."

Emily laughed. "There must be something about the name Kate. That's my mother's name and she's always serious, too."

By now the girls had reached the edge of the garden and the others came running for a drink. Bella poured some of the water into a crockery jug for later and suggested Emma take the remaining water to the men working in the field. Then the sisters went back to hoeing.

"Come on," said Emma. "Now I can introduce you to the rest of my family. You've already seen Grandma and Geordie. He's named after my dad."

"Where are they?"

"Oh, Granny is probably collecting eggs and feeding the chickens. She's partial to them. She says 'if you treat them well, they'll lay better for you.' It's worked so far." Emma laughed. "Geordie's probably gone fishing, or getting into trouble somewhere."

They ducked under the rope clothesline where the laundry was flapping in the wind between two trees, and followed a narrow trail through some scraggly bush. In the clearing ahead Emily could see a man struggling behind a plough and oxen, his shaggy grey hair matted to his neck under his wide-brimmed hat, and a much younger man tugging on the harness of the balking pair of animals. Sweat was pouring off both the men and the huge beasts. The oxen switched their tails frantically to keep the clusters of mosquitoes and flies off their bodies.

"There's my dad, working up some new land. That's Sandy wrestling with the oxen. He's the oldest of us kids. And there's Duncan and Jack." She pointed to two figures at the bottom of the field, one wielding an axe, the other dragging roots over to a pile at the edge of the clearing.

The girls stood watching the scene for a few moments. Emily wiped the sweat from her own forehead and swatted at little flies. How could they work in this heat and with all these bugs? She could hardly stand it, especially when the grasshoppers suddenly whirred and flew up at her. They reminded her of the summer she'd ridden her bike frantically to the potato patch every day with her eyes closed most of the time, while surges of the leaping insects pelted her from all directions.

All at once they heard some loud bellowing from the oxen. The men shouted to each other through the din. Emma's dad was yanking on the reins, while Sandy used a switch to try to keep the oxen from dashing off. But there was no stopping the animals. They jerked the reins out of the men's hands. Duncan and Jack came racing up the field, yelling and waving their arms to head them off, but the cattle made right for a nearby slough, dragging the plough behind them. They didn't halt until they were standing belly deep in the water, where they drank their fill between bellows.

Emily heard a great deal more cussing from the men, as they discussed how to retrieve the oxen and plough, but by the time the girls arrived at the banks of the slough the men were laughing. Duncan and Jack had waded into the water and were splashing each other, while Sandy was yanking on the harness, trying to persuade the animals to come back to shore. Emma's dad was leaning against a tree swatting at the horseflies with his shirt, which he had removed moments before. His face was creased with streaks of dirt and moisture.

"Hello, lass. You've come at a good time," he said in a thick marbly voice as they approached. A stocky, muscular man with red streaks in his greying beard, he gave Emma a wide grin, and Emily could see how Geordie resembled him. "Drat those oxen. They'll not get the better of me and my boys," he laughed, as he shook his fist at them.

He appeared not to see Emily, and she was glad he couldn't. She and Emma would have a great deal of explaining to do. Besides, it was kind of fun being invisible to people.

Plunging the dipper into the pail of water, Emma's dad took a long drink, and poured the rest over his bare head. Then Emma gave him his hat, which had flown off in the chase. By now Sandy had the oxen up on the bank, and the others were walking over for a drink of water from the pail Emma had brought.

Sandy was laughing as he joined them. "That was quite a tussle. Did you see how determined they were?"

Emily clutched her sides with laughter as he acted out the scene again, exaggerating the movements of everyone chasing after the runaway animals. Sandy, although he obviously was strong, was tall and thin, more like his mother. Emily found it hard to believe, when she saw him up close, that he had been able to handle the powerful oxen as well as he had.

Duncan and Jack, rivulets of water streaked through the dust and sweat on their faces, seemed more likely to be the ones that could manage the beasts. They were both sturdy, husky young men. Duncan was bearded like his father and brother Sandy, but Jack was dark-haired and smooth-faced, younger than the others. He looked more serious too.

He seemed anxious to get back to work, and once they'd all had their fill of water, he was the first to return to the field. The oxen were more subdued, but still bawling as they were led back to the plough.

The girls trailed behind the men, and Emma left the pail of water for them in a shaded spot under a tree. Neither of the girls noticed Geordie hidden in the branches above. Nor did they hear him jump down and follow them as they headed back to the rock.

Emma and Emily stopped briefly at the house for a basket, and then hurried through the bluff to the meadow where the boulder stood. There they gathered some camomile. Emily carefully explained to Emma how to brew the tea for her mother, even though Emma thought her granny would know how to do it.

Before they parted at the rock, Emma gave Emily a quick hug. "Thanks for a fine day, lass."

"Thank *you*," Emily replied. She could feel a happy glow on her face as she stood for a few moments watching Emma disappear through the trees. Now she knew what was meant in *Anne of Green Gables* about kindred spirits.

Suddenly Emily realized how incredibly late she must be. Just before she popped the special stone in its hiding place, she thought she caught a movement out of the corner of her eye. But she quickly dismissed it and sped for home. And not until she was turning the knob on the porch door, did she realize she'd forgotten to ask Emma her last name.

CHAPTER SEVEN

"Young lady, where have you been? You were gone for hours," Kate demanded, when she caught sight of Emily sneaking into the kitchen. "And just look at you – you're soaked."

"I sort of lost track of the time," said Emily, staring at her soggy sneakers and jeans. "I was visiting with Emma."

"What else were you doing?" Her mother placed her hands on her hips. "Both Gerald Ferguson and Mrs. Barkley say they saw you cross the pasture and go to the rocks. But then they said you just disappeared, and for the longest time."

Emily looked at her mother through the hair that had fallen over her eyes and saw her mouth tighten. "Well...uh...I was with Emma. But I guess they just didn't see us," she suggested, thoughts tumbling through her head at record speed. Of course, they couldn't have seen her or Emma. But her mother would never believe her if she told the entire truth. How was she going to explain?

"No, they definitely did not see anyone with you, Emily Marie," said her mother with a stern look on her face. "Mr. Ferguson was out in the west field where he had a good view of the spot, too."

Oh, oh, thought Emily. Now what could she say?

"Gerald Ferguson phoned to tell me he'd be picking us up for town at one o'clock. Then he mentioned seeing you, and how you disappeared. I didn't know what to think."

"I did meet Emma," Emily insisted. At least that part was true. "Then I – I guess we were imagining what it must have been like in the old days. You know, when the pioneers first came here," she said, hoping her mother would fall for her story. It was partially true. "We were pretending to look for berries and things."

"You're not going to try and tell me some silly story about time travelling again, are you?"

Emily shook her head. There was no way she was going to tell her mother anything about her experiences with Emma. She'd never understand in a hundred years. At the thought of a hundred years, Emily could feel a bubble of laughter rising. She swallowed hard. She must think of something else. She dropped her head to her chest, still struggling to keep in the laughter. Tears of mirth and anxiety formed in her eyes.

That's when she glanced down at her hands and saw the purple stains on her fingers. In an instant her threatened laughter died. She clamped her hands into tight fists. Oh, no! How was she going to explain about her hands? Was her mouth discoloured too? She kept her head down, letting her hair fall over her face again. Silently she prayed her mother wouldn't notice.

For the moment, Kate was busy explaining how Mrs. Barkley had called right after Gerald Ferguson. She'd seen almost the same thing as he had, and neither one of them had met any new family, although they had heard someone was supposed to be buying the McGuillivray place.

"Edna Barkley couldn't figure out where you went, and wondered if something happened to you." Her mother's expression had changed to one of concern. "I was just about to go looking for you. I thought maybe you'd fallen off a rock or something."

Darn that nosy Mrs. Barkley. Why couldn't the woman mind her own business? Emily would have to be more careful from now on.

To her mother she said, "I'm sorry to worry you, Mom. But I was with Emma, and maybe we were just in one of the gullies. There are lots up there." Sullenly she thought, you'd know if you ever came for a walk with me. Aloud she added, "They probably just couldn't see us."

The crunch of gravel on the driveway sent Kate scurrying over to the window. She waved to someone outside and held up five fingers to indicate they'd be out in a few minutes.

"It's Gerald Ferguson to pick us up. Run and change out of those wet clothes. We'll talk about this later." Kate shuffled some papers together on the table and stuffed them into her briefcase as Emily scampered out of the room. She called after Emily, "And by the way, Em, make sure you wash your hands – they're filthy. And wipe that dirt off your mouth too."

ALL AFTERNOON Emily followed her mother and Gerald Ferguson around town. She was careful not to complain about how long everything was taking at the Credit Union, or to ask for anything in the Co-op grocery store. She tried hard to be agreeable with her mother, and was so convincing that Mr. Ferguson commented on her pleasant manner and suggested they stop at Harry's Café for a piece of pie. He even offered to buy. Her mother consented, since the photos weren't quite ready at the newspaper office and they also had to wait for the last bus to arrive. Gerald Ferguson needed to pick up a part for his tractor.

Emily sighed and followed her mother and Mr. Ferguson to a side booth in the gloomy room. As she sipped on her Coke, she watched them eating rhubarb pie and drinking coffee and wished she were back at her grandmother's place.

She had only until Sunday. Just three days away, and then she'd be back in Regina. After that, she'd hardly have a chance to visit the farm before the auction. She wanted to spend as much time with Emma as she could. And maybe somehow before Sunday, Emily could think of a way to keep the farm.

She slurped the last of the liquid out of the glass and muttered to herself as she tapped her foot against the bench leg. Why couldn't the time go faster? She wanted to be up and moving. Then maybe she could figure things out. She needed to ask Emma her last name.

By the time they'd returned to her grandmother's house it was almost eight o'clock. Dusk was descending into darkness and the first stars flickered overhead. Kate invited Gerald in for supper, but he declined, saying he had chores to do. He disappeared down the lane in a shower of dust, headlights glancing over the pasture as he swung around the corner onto the access road towards his farm three miles away.

Emily helped her mother unpack the groceries, and they fixed a quick supper of leftover stew. By the time they cleaned up the kitchen and stowed the rest of their purchases away, it was almost bedtime. Emily figured her mother might have forgotten about her lateness that morning. Kate had been silent most of the evening, busy filing bank documents into a folder with Grandmother Renfrew's other paperwork.

As Emily grabbed a banana from the fruit bowl to take upstairs with her, she spied the parcel from the newspaper office on the table beside Kate. They'd both forgotten about the photographs. Emily decided they might be the perfect thing to take her mother's mind off any further discussion about her actions that morning.

"Can I see the photos?" she asked, pointing to the package. Her aunt Liz hadn't found the photo album with her grandparent's wedding picture in it before she left, and Emily was curious.

"Oh, sure, Em. I never even had a chance at the newspaper office to see how they turned out." Kate slid the photos out. "Oh, these are good." She passed one to Emily.

"Wow, Grandma is so young in this photo. What a neat dress she's wearing. Don't they look serious, though?"

"They had to be very still. The cameras were different back then and required really long exposures," explained her mother, reaching for the group photo.

Emily came to stand behind her mother and looked at the picture over her shoulder. It was of a family. The parents sat stiff-backed on sturdy chairs and eight children stood around them.

"I don't really recognize anyone," said Kate. "I'm not sure who this would be, but look at the clothes. Those must have been their Sunday best. They usually only had one other set and over them the girls wore p —"

"Pinafores," Emily squawked, glad she was standing behind her mother so Kate couldn't see the startled expression on her face.

"No need to get so excited, Emily," her mother scolded.

Emily stared in silent shock at one of the girls in the photo. It was *Emma*! She'd almost missed her, because she was half hidden behind a boy almost as tall as she was. The boy was Geordie, Emma's impish younger brother. There could be no mistake. As Emily looked closer at the group she realized the photo was of Emma's whole family. Dressed so formally and in a studio setting, she hardly recognized them. But why did Grandmother Renfrew have a photograph of Emma's family?

She was just about to question her mother on that point when the phone rang in the hall. Emily ran to answer, and groaned inwardly. It was Lindsay, her mother's business partner. Now her mother would be talking about work for ages. As Kate picked up the phone, Emily mouthed a request to her mother to take the group photo up to her room. Kate nodded yes, and gave her daughter a quick hug, before Emily went upstairs.

When she reached her bedroom, Emily flung herself on her bed to study the photograph. Everyone she'd met that morning was in it, except Emma's grandmother and sister Molly. Obviously this was taken before they'd come to Canada. This family must have been neighbours or really good friends to her grandparents for them to have the photo.

Emily changed into her nightgown, then opened her window. A full moon illuminated the pasture, and she thought she could hear crickets chirping and soft rustlings on the ground below. A cool breeze filtered through her curtains, chilling her bare arms. As she hopped into bed, Emily realized she didn't know much about her grandparents' history – when they had arrived, and where they had grown up. She knew her grandmother had been born in the North-West Territories and had been raised somewhere in this area, but she wasn't sure exactly where. And so many of the older people in the community had been born before Saskatchewan was made into a province in 1905. No clue there.

She'd have to ask her mother, but she knew Kate was much younger than the others, a last child born when Grandmother Renfrew was in her forties, and she had never taken any interest in family history. I know, thought Emily, I'll take this photograph to Emma tomorrow when I go to ask her about her last name. Maybe she can tell me how come my grandmother had the photograph.

Yawning, she inserted the portrait into her notebook and slid it back under the window ledge. She decided she was too tired to write in her journal. She crawled into bed and promptly went to sleep.

EMMA WASN'T AT THE ROCK when Emily arrived the next morning. She'd crept out when the sun was just barely rising over the horizon, planning to make this a quick trip and return before her mother awoke. Of course it was early, and Emma probably couldn't come to the rock every day.

After a few moments' hesitation, Emily decided to go find Emma instead of waiting for her. She reached for the stone in the crevice, and slipped into Emma's world with hardly a tremor.

Walking quickly along the well-worn trail through the bush, Emily realized this was the first time she'd gone to Emma's homestead alone. Although she felt a bit nervous, she was positive she'd find her way. The poplar leaves rustled as they twisted in the brisk wind, and this time there were no insects to pester her. The day was cool, and Emily was glad she'd thought to wear a jacket. It was also a good place to carry the photo.

As she approached the clearing, she discovered Emma's mother outside. She was scrubbing laundry on a washboard in a wooden tub, sheltered from the wind on the west side of the house. As Emily passed by Emma's mother, she thought she heard her humming, but couldn't tell above the swishing sounds of the grass blowing in the wind.

She found Emma on the other side of the yard, scurrying back and forth checking the washing on the line. The clothes snapped in the stiff breeze.

"Psst," Emily called to her from behind a tree.

Startled, Emma almost dropped the willow basket, but grinned when she saw Emily.

"Got you back." Emily laughed, poking Emma playfully in the arm.

"Yes, that you did, lass." Emma chuckled, and set the load of laundry on the ground.

"I see your mother is feeling better."

"Yes, thanks to you, Emily. That camomile tea was splendid. Granny has been giving it to us all." Emma removed pegs and plucked the dried clothes from the line.

"I'm glad it worked," Emily said. Suddenly remembering why she'd come, she handed Emma the picture. "I can't stay. I just wanted to show you this."

Emma stared at the photo and looked up at Emily in surprise. "That's my family! We took this picture in Glasgow before we left Scotland."

"I thought so. But if this is your family, why do you think my grandmother had the negative?" Emily held her breath as she waited for Emma's answer.

"I don't know." A puzzled expression crossed Emma's face.

"Emma!" All at once Emma's mother was calling. "What's taking you so long, lass? I've another load ready to be hung up."

"I've got to run, Emily, but we'll try and figure it out next time we're together." She squeezed Emily's hand, then dashed off. Her braids slapped against her back as she ran.

"Wait!" yelled Emily. "At least tell me what your last name is."

"Elliott," Emma called back.

Elliott. Something jangled in the back of Emily's mind. Wasn't Elliott her grandmother's maiden name? Were they related somehow? She knew whole groups of pioneer families often immigrated together and settled in the same areas. Maybe that's what had happened.

Emily started running back up the trail to the rock. She'd have to hurry to get back before her mother woke up.

WHEN EMILY RETURNED to the yard, her aunt Liz's car was parked out front. Darn, now they'd know she'd been gone. But why was Aunt Liz back?

"Morning, Em," said her mother abruptly, when she stepped into the kitchen. "I see you've been back out to those rocks. We still haven't had our little talk about your behaviour yesterday, have we?"

"Hi, Mom," said Emily, clenching her fingers at her sides and trying to figure out what to say. Maybe it would be best to ignore her mother for the time being. She turned to her aunt. "Hi, Aunt Liz, what are you doing here?"

"I just couldn't let your mother do all this sorting herself, so I put Roger in charge at the office and took more time off. Roger will be taking over anyway when I retire, so he can handle it. And, well, here I am." Aunt Liz smiled at Emily, then looked quizzically at mother and daughter. Her blue eyes held a question, but she kept it to herself.

"She's here until Sunday," added Kate.

"How did you get here so early?" Emily asked. She grabbed an apple from the bowl on the table and polished it on her pants before taking a bite.

Aunt Liz had come most of the way the previous night, but decided not to disturb Emily and her mom so late. She'd stopped forty miles away at the Whitewood motel around one in the morning.

"The water pipes were clanging by six and I couldn't sleep any more, so I got up and drove here." Laughing, Liz reached for the coffee pot on the stove and poured Kate and herself another cup.

As she crunched on her apple, Emily was amazed at how energetic her sixty-four-year-old aunt was after having so little sleep. She and her mother were already planning their work for the day. Emily glanced at the clock. It wasn't even eight o'clock yet. She sidled towards the hallway.

"Your dad called while you were gone."

"Aw." Emily groaned, stopping short. Darn, she was sorry she'd missed her father's call. "What did he say?"

"He says hello and sends his love, but we'll have to manage without him for awhile. He's going to be gone a little longer than he expected." Kate whisked some crumbs off the counter and shook the dishrag into the sink. Then she began polishing the taps. "He'll phone again in a couple of days."

"Oh, good." Emily turned towards the hall-way again, trying to slink out of the room.

"So what *were* you doing, Emily?" asked her mother.

The sudden question brought Emily to a halt again. "I just went out for a walk." She unzipped her jacket, and flicked her hair over her shoulder. The photograph slipped to the floor. She'd forgotten about it.

"What are you doing with that picture?" asked Kate, puzzled.

"Uh, I thought Emma might like to see it," she answered, quickly retrieving it. She hoped she wouldn't have to explain everything.

"Let's see it," said Aunt Liz, taking it from her. "Oh, you did get those negatives developed. Gee, I'm not sure who all these people are, but they look vaguely familiar."

"I thought you'd know," said Kate, nudging her sister's elbow. "You're so much older than me."

"Well I *don't* know, and I'm not *that* old," laughed Aunt Liz. "But you could ask your aunt Maggie if she knows, Emily. She'll be here on Sunday. She's the oldest of us *kids*." Aunt Liz poked Kate back, "Not me."

Emily laughed. Her mom and aunt were always joking about their ages. Aunt Liz, ten years older than Kate, was going to retire sometime next year. Kate always teased her sister by saying she'd never feel old enough to retire, because having Emily so late in her life kept her young.

Emily realized she'd never thought of her mother as being older, maybe because Kate was so much younger than all her brothers and sisters. Grandma Renfrew had been in her forties when Kate had been born, and Kate in turn had been in her forties when she'd had Emily. Aunt Maggie, the oldest of all Grandma Renfrew's family, was already in her seventies, and Emily agreed that Aunt Maggie would probably know the people in the photograph.

Emily held the picture up. "Gee, could I keep this one?"

"Well, I don't know," said her mother, looking at Aunt Liz for help.

"Just for now?" Emily pleaded.

"How about you can keep it until you talk to your Aunt Maggie on Sunday. Then when we find out who all these people are, and if they're related, we'll get some more copies made and you can have one for yourself, okay?" Aunt Liz patted Emily's back and handed her the photograph.

"Okay." Emily smiled and raced upstairs to hide the picture under the window ledge.

FOR THE REST OF THE DAY Emily helped her mom and aunt finish cleaning out the attic. Kate explained to

Liz about the arrangements she'd just made with Gerald Ferguson to keep renting the land for the rest of the year. He was to seed the crops and harvest them. In the fall the place would be put up for sale, but sometime before this summer they'd have the auction.

Emily helped her mother and aunt carry some of Grandmother Renfrew's special belongings into one of the bedrooms. These were the articles they thought some of the other family members would like as keepsakes. Everything else was to be sold. Emily helped haul the items to the granaries outside, except for the cushioned chairs, footstools, and other fabric-covered pieces that might be damaged by mice. These they left in the enclosed veranda on the main floor.

Emily's hands were kept busy, but her mind worked overtime trying to figure out how Emma's family could possibly be linked to hers. She was certain they had to be associated in some way, certain her own grandmother's name had been Elliott, and that her family had originally come from Scotland too.

Her mother and Aunt Liz confirmed this when she asked them at lunch time, but they didn't know what other family members had immigrated to the same area in those years. Disappointed by their lack of interest and knowledge, Emily left them on the second floor while she inspected the attic once more.

Next time Emily saw Emma, she'd question her closely about her background, and the possibility of other family members joining them. Maybe together they'd figure out the connection.

CHAPTER EIGHT

Emily never had the opportunity to ask Emma about family connections the next day. In fact, the other girl barely had time to acknowledge her arrival. And Emily was stunned by what she saw.

Everything was quiet and still when she neared the homestead. Even the air was calm, and the drone of the insects hushed as she tramped along the trail through the bush. She noticed a change in the seasons again; the sun angled lower to the ground, and goldenrod and yarrow bloomed by the waysides. Autumn colours tinged the overhanging leaves, and the wild grass was bowed and faded as she walked through the tangled clumps.

When she reached the clearing, there was no sign of human activity in the yard or garden. Only the animals languished in their pens. There was an occasional squeal from a piglet and the mild clucking of hens as they foraged for food in the underbrush. But today, there were no sounds of axes ringing in the thicket beyond, nor shouts of motivation to the sluggish oxen.

Cautiously, Emily approached the house. She thought she heard whimpering inside. She peeked between the slats in the shutters and she caught sight of Jack and Sandy on the other side of the cabin floor. Both writhed in pain on their straw mattresses. Geordie moaned in a corner where he was curled up in a blanket, clutching his stomach. On a cot along the back wall of the hut, Emma's grandmother lay still. Although Kate and Bella appeared to be asleep, Emily sensed that none of the occupants seemed aware of their surroundings. Except Emma.

As she pressed a cloth to her mother's forehead with one hand, she rocked the baby's cradle with the other in an attempt to stop the little mite's crying. Emily saw the beads of moisture on Emma's pinched face, and the exhaustion that sapped her body.

Just then Emma's father groaned on the bed where he lay beside his wife. Emma reached out to feel his forehead, then scuttled over to a basin on the table. Wringing out another cloth, she rushed back and laid it across her father's brow.

Emily watched Emma go to the woodbox, find it empty, then head for the door. When Emma stepped outside, Emily called gently to her from the side of the house.

"Emma. It's me. What's happened?" She touched Emma's arm.

Emma crumpled against her, and sobbed. "Oh, Emily. Everyone has some sort of sickness. I think they caught it from the people who came through here a few days ago."

Emily hugged Emma to her. As the girl wept Emily gently rubbed her tight shoulders. At last Emma's shaking sobs subsided. A few moments later she straightened up and wiped her damp face with her apron.

Then she explained as she pulled Emily towards the woodpile. A caravan of covered wagons with a dozen families immigrating from England were travelling farther west. Many of them had been sick and some had died on the trail. They'd picked up some sort of influenza in Manitoba, but they'd thought they were over it when they stopped with Emma's family to rest.

Emily shuddered at Emma's story. The thought of people sick and dying with no doctor available for miles around appalled her. How sad to think of people being buried in some strange land while their families left them and moved on. It was so different from Grandmother Renfrew's funeral with all the relatives and friends gathered around. And knowing she could visit her grandmother's gravesite easily seemed comforting in comparison.

As Emma continued the story, the girls filled the wheelbarrow with split wood from the huge woodpile. They worked quickly, knowing the needs of the people inside the sod house depended on them. As she tried to grasp what Emma told her, Emily could hear Molly's faint cries through the stillness of the day.

The Elliotts had offered fresh water and food to the travel-weary bunch, and a place to rest and do laundry while they regained their strength to continue their trip. Then, on the second night of their stay, one of the little boys had fallen ill. The family left immediately for Wolseley, twenty miles away, in search of the doctor they'd heard was there.

"We didn't know how to help them," said Emma, grabbing a stick of wood and throwing it into the nearby wheelbarrow with more force than was necessary. "And Wolseley is too far away travelling with oxen. I don't think they could have gotten there in time to save the wee child."

"But the worst...." Emma took in a deep breath and looked skyward as tears threatened to overtake her again. She continued in a shaky voice, "The worst thing is...that my family is sick now, and I don't know what to do."

Emily hugged Emma again to her, trying to comfort the distraught girl. All the while her mind was reeling at the implications. She remembered vaguely hearing about flu epidemics from history classes at school, and something her grandmother had said once. But she didn't have any idea how to help. She only knew she *had* to help. Emma's whole family was in grave danger.

A soft breeze began to blow, and overhead in the trees the song of a meadowlark seemed to calm Emma.

"What have you tried so far?" Emily asked gently, her arms still around the quivering girl's shoulders.

Emma recounted the symptoms and her actions. Chills and then high fevers and delirium. Some had stomach cramps and nausea. She'd combatted them as best she could by keeping a hot fire going in the house and placing cool compresses on everyone stricken. She'd kept them all covered with blankets, except to wash them. She'd fed them a vegetable broth and tea. But there were just too many of them sick, and she'd run out of camomile and hadn't had time to pick more.

"I have to keep running out for firewood and water," Emma said. "There's never enough."

Emily could see the circles of fatigue under Emma's eyes, the pallor and thinness of her body. "I can see you haven't had enough sleep either." She helped Emma push the clumsy wheelbarrow along the narrow bumpy track.

What could she do to help? If only she could remember what her grandmother had taught her about medicinal plants. Emily knew there was a book back at the stone house that might help, but if she returned for it, she knew she'd be too late. The time changed too quickly in Emma's world.

Just then the wheelbarrow toppled over, spilling all the wood. The girls cried out in dismay. Then quickly they righted the heavy conveyance and loaded it up again. As Emily scrambled for a couple of blocks she felt something scrape her arm. She winced and examined the scratch, then looked down at the brambles lying trampled on the ground. *Rose bushes.* Of course.

Emily grabbed Emma's hand excitedly, and pointed to the little red berries on the prickly stems. "There's our answer. Rosehips!"

"What?" Emma looked at Emily through dull, tired eyes.

"There are tons of vitamins in these berries. They can't hurt. We'll make a tea from them," Emily explained. "Come on. I'll help you get this wood in, and you go for water while I pick some of these."

They pushed the wheelbarrow hard and it rumbled towards the house. Emily didn't even wonder if the other occupants thought it strange that pieces of wood were flying into the woodbox seemingly unaided. Everyone was too sick to notice or remember if they did notice. She continued to help Emma fill the box, then grabbed a basket off a shelf and headed back outside with Emma at her heels.

Emma's steps seemed to quicken and her spirits improve as she headed for the well. When she returned, Emily brought the berries into the house and helped Emma brew the tea. While it was steeping, Emily rocked Molly to sleep in her cradle, then began wringing out fresh cloths so that Emma could wipe the sweating brows.

She helped Emma wherever she could. At one point she laid a cool hand across Geordie's forehead. She was startled to see his eyes pop open.

"Are you an angel?" he asked, a blissful grin on his face as he stared up at her. In his delirious state he seemed to be able to see her.

Emily just smiled, and Geordie dozed. Sometime afterwards his fever seemed to break and he rested more easily, drifting into an almost normal sleep. Once Emma was able to spoon tea into everyone else's mouths, they settled more comfortably. Later Emily insisted Emma rest for awhile.

"I'll keep watch and if I need you, I'll call," she assured Emma. The other girl plunked herself into the rocking chair, and instantly nodded off.

Emily was too overwrought to rest. Her mind shuffled through remedies and instructions she'd learned over the years from Grandmother Renfrew. She'd spent many hours wandering the meadows and hills of her grandparents' farm, listening as her grandmother rattled off the names of each plant and the properties they provided for natural healing. Emily had even gathered some, dried them, and then labelled them in a notebook, but that didn't do her any good now. If only she could remember which ones to pick! Maybe if she were outside it would come back more easily.

Noting that Emma was wakening again at the sound of Molly's whimpers, Emily motioned to her friend that she was going back out to pick more rosehips and camomile. As she gathered the berries and flowers into the basket she'd brought along, Emily looked about her at the surrounding vegetation. She knew the plants and trees were filled with good nutrients and medicine.

Suddenly remembering the sweltering day she'd seen the oxen escape to the slough, she thought of the willows that draped over the banks. White willow bark – that's what she needed. Emily grabbed her basket and ran to the slough, mumbling instructions to herself on how to prepare the mixture. It was important to remember exact proportions, or they could be harmful instead of helpful.

Emily quickly found a stand of the right trees and stripped a little bark off the base of several trunks, using a sharp stick to get it started. This proved to be too slow, so she broke several branches off and stuck them into the basket.

More remedies were surfacing in her mind as she worked. Raspberry leaves and the inside of poplar bark. Even sage and stinging nettle would be good. Emily practically flew about the area gathering every kind of plant, root or berry she could think of that might help. As she worked, she went over the recipes in her mind, knowing it was vital to use the proper amounts of each and to prepare them correctly.

Rushing back to the cabin, she lifted the latch softly and opened the door. Emma was weeping.

"It's Granny," she whispered hoarsely. "She's dying. I know it."

Emily tiptoed over to the cot where Emma's grand-mother lay. Her skin was yellow and her breath came in great rasps with a lingering rattle in her chest. Emily could feel the hair stand up at the nape of her own neck. The old woman looked just like Grandmother Renfrew had before she'd died.

Emma came to stand beside her, and Emily clasped Emma's hands in hers. Both girls stood wide-eyed as Granny struggled for breath, and then after a huge gasp was silent. It was over so quickly that the girls never even had a chance to do anything. Numb, Emily pulled the blanket up over the old woman's face, then drew the sobbing Emma outside.

IT SEEMED LIKE AGES LATER that Emma finally stirred. She'd fallen asleep with her head cradled in Emily's lap. Emily must have dozed too, for the sun was lower in the sky and a breeze wafted through the clearing. She felt chilled and cramped.

Just then they heard the door latch opening behind them, and both girls scrambled to their feet. Sandy stumbled out and headed to the bushes behind the house where they could hear him being sick. A few moments later he reappeared, trembling and shaky on his feet.

Emma ran to him. "Come, you must get back to bed."

"No. We have to bury Granny," he mumbled.

"We can do it later," Emma insisted. "When some of the others can help." She grabbed Sandy by the shoulder.

But he shrugged her off and staggered to the barn for a shovel.

They found him collapsed there a few minutes later. Emma roused him and together she and Emily managed to help him to the house. Emily held open the door. Then he sank onto his mattress moaning. At the commotion, Geordie sat up.

Emily huddled by the door, not sure if she wanted to venture in very far with the lifeless form lying on the other side of the room. Instead, she watched Emma give Geordie some broth when he said he was feeling better. Soon after, he slept again.

The girls quickly scooped up the neglected basket of herbs and plants, a basin and a knife, and took them outside to the plank bench on the east side of the house. There they began preparing the ingredients needed for the remedies. They separated and washed leaves and roots, and scraped inner bark from its casings. As they worked, Emily explained the uses of the plants and how to make various medicines.

Once Emma took a few minutes to feed and water the animals. When she returned to Emily's side, they talked quietly about their lives. At first they avoided mentioning Emma's grandmother's death. Emily was concerned about Emma's reaction, but Emma was the first to bring up the subject. She mentioned how odd it was that they'd both lost their grandmothers so recently.

Emma seemed to be consoled by being able to share her feelings with Emily, because she understood so well.

Emily soon learned what a feisty and hardy lady the senior Mrs. Elliott had really been. She had raised five children alone after her young husband had died falling off a roof he was thatching for a neighbour. For years they had struggled, living in a tiny hut on rough hilly terrain, but somehow she'd always managed to have food on the table for her growing brood.

Emily thought of all the modern conveniences she had available to her in comparison to the primitive life of the Elliotts. How difficult everything must have been for them. Emily looked at the rough-hewn plank she and Emma were working on behind the squat sod house. Perhaps their daily life as immigrants wasn't much different from what they'd known in Scotland.

They weren't even property owners, according to Emma, just renters. And when their lord of the manor had decided to sell and break up his estate, all the renters were homeless. They lost the small plots of land that they'd lived on for generations, and would never be able to go back, nor have any hope of owning land them-selves if they did.

Even though the elder Mrs. Elliott loved her "bonnie" Scotland, she'd been willing to emigrate to a new country with her youngest son and his family. At least they had a chance of owning their own land. And the other members of her family would be following soon.

The girls continued to clean and chop roots as Emma talked. Emily was spellbound by Emma's account. The probable sale of Grandmother Renfrew's farm seemed minor in comparison to the upset the Elliotts had faced. They weren't even able to live in their own country. At least Emily was staying on the prairies and could easily take a drive through the land she loved so much. She shook her head, realizing she had many reasons to be thankful.

"Why are you looking so queer?" Emma asked, setting down the knife she'd been using on the willow branches.

Emily shrugged. "I was just thinking about how different your life is from mine. Yet how similar in a way."

She threw a basinful of dirty water onto the ground, and then walked over to the rain barrel at the corner of the house. As she scooped clean water into the bowl and dropped more roots in to soak, she told Emma about the auction and sale of Grandmother Renfrew's farm. Emily also explained all the ideas she had for saving the farm, but none seemed realistic when she discussed them with her friend.

Her family didn't seem to want to be bothered with renting the land to Gerald Ferguson, because of the problems of having to split the proceeds between all the family members, and her uncle Ian wasn't going to come out of retirement to run it either. None of the other family members who farmed lived near enough to make it feasible to work the land along with their own. There seemed no hope for keeping her grandmother's beloved farm.

All of a sudden Emily gasped. She'd forgotten all about going home. She'd been so caught up in Emma's world that she'd been gone from her own for ages. "We'd better get some of these things steeping, Emma. I've got to get back."

Gathering a handful of herbs and leaves, she rushed into the house and began measuring them into a pot. As she poured boiling water over them, she explained to Emma again what the various ingredients did. In another bowl she prepared a liniment to rub on their chests, hoping she'd remembered just exactly how her grandmother had prepared it. She'd seen Grandmother Renfrew do some of these things many times, but it was different when she had to do it herself. At least she knew none of the ingredients were toxic and if she'd put a little too much of one thing in, it wouldn't harm the Elliots.

"Are you sure you can remember all that?" Emily quizzed Emma anxiously when she was done. "Make sure you follow what I said exactly, otherwise it might not work."

Emma nodded and recited the information back to Emily as she laid each plant or root from the basket onto the table. Confident the girl understood, Emily headed for the door. "I'll be back as soon as I can. Good luck." She ran back and gave Emma a hug.

"Thanks for all your help, Emily," Emma whispered into her ear. "You're the best friend I could ever have."

Emma watched Emily walk across the room. Her eyes were full of admiration. "Good-bye, lass."

"Good-bye, Emma. Take care of yourself. See you soon."

As Emily reached the door, Molly let out a healthy cry and Emma's mother awoke. Emily watched through the almost closed door as the woman sat up shakily on the edge of the cot and tried reaching for the unhappy child.

"You're awake?" Emma ran and hugged her mother. Then she picked up Molly. As she placed the squawking baby in her mother's arms, Geordie and Sandy stirred at the noise. Emma turned and gave Emily a smile that said "everything is going to be all right now."

Emily closed the door softly and darted for home through the quickly failing light. When she reached the rock, she yanked the stone from her pocket and deposited it back in the crevice. With a jolt she found herself in total darkness.

Instant terror gripped Emily. She could feel the fear all the way from her scalp to the pit of her stomach. She'd never been this far from the house this late at night. Not only that, she had no idea how long she'd been gone, or how much trouble she'd be in when she got home.

Squinting to get her eyes adjusted to the darkness, she stumbled down the slope in what she hoped was the right direction. Gradually as she walked, the moon seemed to brighten the starlit sky, and she could see the trampled grass of a path in front of her. She quickened her pace when she heard the distant howl of a coyote.

The evening was damp and chilly, and she felt numbed by the events of the day. Exhaustion was closing in on her, and halfway across the pasture, she tripped and fell. Shortly afterwards she heard a rustling in the buckbrush. She must have disturbed some creature. She shuddered and jumped back up to her feet, not wanting to guess what it might have been. A rabbit, she told herself and ran.

By now she could make out a faint glow in one of the windows of the stone house ahead, but it was odd the place wasn't lit up more. She found it even stranger when she finally crawled through the pasture fence into the yard and discovered there was a light only in the kitchen.

Cautiously she opened the porch door to the chirping of crickets close at hand. She couldn't hear any sound inside, except the hum of the fridge. At the table a hastily scribbled note in Aunt Liz's handwriting leaned against a vase of flowers.

Another shot of adrenalin pulsed through Emily's body as she read how her mother had fallen and injured her wrist. Aunt Liz had taken her to have it X-rayed at the hospital in town, but they didn't know when they'd return. Except that it would be sometime tonight. Emily was to call either the Fergusons or the Barkleys, if she needed anything.

Emily wilted into a chair. At least her mom probably wouldn't know how long she'd been gone. But she wondered how badly her mom was hurt. How had the accident happened? Emily laid her head on the table. She didn't think she could take any more emotional upheavals today. As she lay there calming down, she felt herself almost nod off to sleep. Then she jerked her head up. She had to get up to bed.

As she pulled herself to her feet, she realized she was hungry. She hadn't eaten all day. Yet when she opened the fridge, the only thing that appealed to her was a glass of milk. Emily downed it and dragged her weary body up the stairs.

As she passed the spare room on the second floor, she had an overwhelming desire to take her grandmother's handmade quilt with her. Lethargically, she pulled the quilt off the top shelf of the closet and carried it up the last flight of stairs. Flopping onto the bed, she kicked off her runners, dragged the quilt over her, and fell into an exhausted sleep.

Some time later, she heard the vague sounds of her mother and aunt returning. Emily remembered crawling under the rest of her covers before they came up to her room to tell her everything was fine and to say good night. But she wasn't sure if she'd answered them. She drifted back to sleep, feeling relieved that her mother had only a sprain and hopeful that Emma's family was recovering.

CHAPTER NINE

Emily slept soundly most of the night, but awakened with a start just before dawn. Although still a little groggy from her ordeal of the day before, she felt an urgent need to find out how Emma's family was doing. Quickly she changed into fresh clothes and ran a brush through her hair. Folding the quilt, she tiptoed down the stairs and slid it back into the closet, being as quiet as she could.

Minutes later she slipped out of the house and jogged across the pasture. A stiff breeze made her pull her jacket closer about her. She could hear faint twitterings in the trees as she passed, and by the time she reached the rock, the dark sky was tinged with colour.

With taut fingers she reached for the stone, and found herself shifted into early afternoon and a hazy sky. Although the sun warmed her body, she still felt tense and worried as she walked down the familiar path through the stand of poplars. Her throat tightened as she approached the clearing where Emma's home stood. What would she find there?

A bubble of laughter burst from Emily when she spotted Emma sitting with Molly on a quilt in front of the house. She was braiding onions. In the garden, Emma's mother and sisters were digging rows of potatoes and carrots, laying them in the sun to dry. She could hear oxen bellowing and the shouts of the men in the field in the distance. How wonderful to find things back to normal again in Emma's world!

Geordie suddenly emerged from a deep hole in the ground on the west side of the house, and Emily felt her face break into a grin. He was always popping up from somewhere, and she was glad to see he was active and healthy again. A wheelbarrow heaped with cabbages stood by the entrance. Geordie was probably hauling them down to the root cellar for the family's winter use.

Emily crossed the yard to join Emma, who hadn't noticed her yet. The baby gurgled and pointed as she approached, making her sister glance up. Emma jumped up and ran to meet Emily. They swung each other around and hugged.

"Oh, I'm so glad to see you, lass," said Emma, coughing a little and trying to catch her breath.

Emily could hear a slight wheezing in Emma's chest as she hugged her again. She drew back and looked at her friend. "Are you okay?" Emma looked pale and drawn, thinner.

"I'm fine. I've just a silly cough that won't go away. Come. Sit with us, if you have time." She turned back and settled beside Molly, who was trying to stuff dirt into her mouth. "No, no, little lass. The soil is not meant for you to eat," she murmured to the child.

Emily joined them and distracted Molly by blowing on a blade of grass between her thumbs. Molly obviously could sense Emily's presence just as Emma could, and the strange trumpet-like sound made the baby laugh. She crawled towards Emily. But Emma grabbed her and set her back in the shade.

"Looks like everyone's recovered. Am I right?" Emily grinned at her friend.

"Yes, we're all fine. Thanks to your wonderful brews, Emily." Emma laughed, and sputtered into a handkerchief from her apron pocket as another fit of coughing overtook her.

Emily looked at Emma uncertainly, but the girl waved at her and nodded that she was all right. "I'm just so glad I was in time to help…." Emily's thoughts turned to Emma's granny. At least she'd helped most of them. The rest of her sentence went unspoken.

After a few silent moments, Emma told Emily how they'd buried her grandmother the next morning after Emily had left. By then Sandy, Geordie, and her father were well enough to do it. They laid her to rest on the far edge of their homestead quarter in the shade of some aspen trees on a little rise. She was near enough for

Emma to visit whenever she wished. Emily felt good about this, especially for Emma's sake.

"Wha-hoo!" The yell came from around the corner of the house. In the next instant a salamander came flying through the air. It landed on Emma's lap. With a yelp, she grabbed the lizard-like creature by its tail and jumped to her feet. Emily watched in amazement as Emma tore after Geordie, who was laughing as he raced towards the slough. He was too fast for Emma though, and she soon gave up, throwing the small amphibian into the bush.

She returned slowly; the last few minutes of exertion seemed to have been too much for her. In horror, Emily watched Emma collapse into a coughing fit at her feet.

"Emma, how long have you had this dreadful cough?" she asked in alarm.

"Only a couple of weeks. I'm all right. Really." Emma gasped for breath, trying to evade Emily's stare.

But Emily could see a flash of fear come unbidden into Emma's eyes just before she bent to retrieve Molly. As they talked, Emily couldn't dismiss the feeling of anxiety that was niggling at her solar plexus. Emma was obviously rundown from caring for her sick family, and it was doubtful that she'd had much opportunity to rest since.

As Emily handed Molly some pebbles to admire, she gently reminded Emma to keep preparing some of the herbal tonics that would help relieve her cough. She also suggested several other mixtures that might help. Emma promised to try them.

"I've told Mum how to make all the plant remedies you showed me," added Emma softly. "She thinks I learned them from Granny. Or that I have a natural talent."

The girls chuckled together, and then it was time for Emily to go home. Emma seemed reluctant for Emily to leave. Quickly scooping up Molly, she told Emily she would accompany her back to the rock.

They found the trail through the bluff easier to walk along now that the foliage was spent and falling to the ground. The sky had cleared, and the wind was calm in the bright autumn sun. An occasional bee droned lazily across their path. Underfoot, leaves crunched, and a hawk sailed high above the trees.

As they emerged onto the meadow, Emma exclaimed in joy at the Indian paintbrush and the last vestiges of yarrow and foxtails that grew around the base of the rock. She hadn't been to their special place in ages, she said.

The girls stood looking over the valley, breathing deeply as they watched a huge flock of geese rise from the far marsh and soar towards the south. Molly giggled and clapped her hands at the great honking chorus as the waterfowl passed directly overhead. The girls clapped with her; then Emma set the child on the ground.

Emma clung to Emily a long time when they hugged good-bye. Emily felt a strong kinship and affection pass between them. "Take care, Emma," she whispered, worried about her friend's health.

"You too, lass. You've been a godsend to me and my family." Then she bent and gathered the baby in her arms. "Good-bye," she called, her voice cracking.

Emily felt tears begin to roll down her cheeks as she watched Emma and Molly disappear into the trees. But she didn't know why.

A moment later she heard Emma shriek. "Geordie, you scamp. What are you doing spying on me like this?"

"I only came to find you," he protested. "Mum was looking for you. What do you do out here all the time, anyway?"

Giggling in relief, Emily wiped the dampness from her face with the back of her hand. Geordie sure could be a pest sometimes. She deposited the stone back into its special place and set out for home.

EMILY MANAGED TO RETURN without her mother and aunt's knowledge, and even had the breakfast table set when they awoke. Her mother appreciated her thoughtfulness, especially now that she wouldn't be able to do as much with her right hand out of commission. However, Emily soon discovered that this minor problem didn't stop Kate from finding things for her and Aunt Liz to do whenever she couldn't do them herself.

"Yes, Ma'am." Emily and Aunt Liz saluted Kate and moved the trunk farther against one wall of the attic. "Does this suit you, Ma'am?"

Kate grimaced at the pair. "That's just fine." She crossed the room and picked up a small box.

"And what would you like us to do with this dresser, Your Highness?" Aunt Liz made a sweeping bow before Kate, who sat on a chair by the head of the stairs. She was sorting through some jewellery.

Kate sighed and pointed beside the trunk.

Emily followed Aunt Liz's example and marched over to her mother. Scarves were draped over her arms and she held them out for Kate's inspection. "Your Majesty. Would these be of any use to you?" She bowed low and the scarves dropped into a colourful heap on the floor. Emily giggled as she and Aunt Liz bonked heads trying to retrieve them.

"I think that's about enough, you two," Kate said through clenched teeth.

"Have we angered Your Highness? Oh, what shall become of us?" Emily and Aunt Liz raised their hands in front of their faces in mock terror.

"I said, cut it out." Kate raised her voice, then calmed down somewhat. "Okay, okay. I know I can be a bit of a dictator at times, but I think you two can understand why I'm not in the best of moods."

"Yeah, I guess so." Emily shrugged her shoulders, and looked over at Aunt Liz.

"Sure we can," Aunt Liz agreed, smiling. "It's not every day you sprain a wrist." Then almost in a whisper she said, "Thank heavens." And she winked at Emily. A little louder, she added, "Anyone who isn't watching where they're going and falls off a grain bin step is allowed to be a grouch."

"I'm not a grouch," Kate protested over the laughter of the other two.

"Yes, you are, Mom. Lighten up." Emily grinned at her.

Kate scowled, but said very little for the rest of the morning, other than to grunt an assent or bark out a "no" to some question one of them asked.

The sky became overcast and it began drizzling around noon. Aunt Liz decided to drive to town for the mail while Kate took a painkiller and had a nap. Emily turned down her aunt's invitation to go along and escaped to her room. She wrote in her journal for a while, going over her experiences with Emma. But she soon found herself lying on the bed worrying instead.

She felt like she'd weathered a whole lifetime with the pioneer girl in just the few days since she'd known her. By now, Emily was fairly certain that Grandmother Renfrew might belong to one of the other branches of the Elliott family that Emma had said would be immigrating in a few months. As she thought about asking

Emma more about her extended family, Emily wondered how Emma was feeling. She drifted into a fitful sleep with images of the farm, her grandmother, and Emma all rolled into one.

She awoke sometime later and noted how quiet the house seemed. Tiptoeing down to her mother's bedroom, she was surprised to find Kate lounging in bed with a book propped up on her chest. Emily couldn't recall her mother ever doing such a thing.

"Hi, Em. I haven't rested in the afternoon like this for years," she said dreamily. "It's kind of nice."

Emily agreed, as she sat on the window seat by the bed. She snuggled into the pillows when she realized her mother felt like chatting.

"I'm sorry for being so irritable earlier, Em. Guess I was just feeling sorry for myself."

"That's okay," Emily replied. "Guess your wrist must hurt a bit, huh?"

"Yeah, kind of." She looked at her bandaged wrist. "But I feel better now."

"Good." Emily felt closer to her mother than she had in a long time, but the silence between them now made her a little shy.

When Kate spoke again she had a wry smile on her face. "I've been thinking, Em. You were right. I do need to take some time for myself once in a while. And spend some time with you too. Maybe later we could take a walk. What do you say?"

"That would be great, Mom." Emily was astonished at the change in her mother. Of course, this also put a damper on Emily's plans for visiting Emma again that day, but she wasn't going to miss this opportunity to spend some time with her mom. If she seemed reluctant to go, Kate might never offer again.

By mid-afternoon the rain stopped and a bright sun beamed through the clouds. Emily was still awed by her mother's decision to go for a walk, but gladly donned rubber boots and set out with Kate across the pasture. She was amazed to discover her mother actually knew the names of wildflowers and some of the other plants.

"Every time I stepped out the door your grand-mother was telling me the names of everything. I guess some of it must have sunk in," said Kate, stooping to pick a feathery dandelion head. She blew it at Emily, and grinned as the seeds parachuted into the sky.

They had a contest then, with Emily winning because her mother couldn't pick fast enough with her uninjured left hand. "No fair," Kate called finally. "I give up."

They walked along the grassy trail in silence for awhile. They almost went as far as the rock, but Emily steered her mother away. She didn't want to take any chances of something weird occurring and having to explain. They were having a pleasant time. At least Kate seemed to be enjoying it. She was smiling and her face looked relaxed.

"Mom, how come you don't usually seem to like it out in the country?" Emily blurted out. Then wished she hadn't asked. She didn't want to break their congenial mood.

Kate turned to Emily in surprise. "But I do, Em. Maybe only in small doses, but I do like to visit the farm once in awhile." Kate seemed to mull Emily's question over. "I guess because I grew up here, I kind of take it for granted. It's just not as special to me as it is for you."

"I suppose." Emily wasn't sure she understood her mother's reasoning.

"I guess there wasn't much of a future here for me. Then when I went away to the city to university and met your father, I knew there was no coming back."

"But don't you feel special when you're out here?" Emily took a deep breath and swung around with her arms outstretched. "This is so wonderful. I could stay here forever."

A strange look of wistfulness came over Kate's face as she watched Emily spin around. "I wish I felt the same way about the prairies as you do. But I just don't." Kate patted Emily's hand. "You know, you're very much like your Grandmother Renfrew in that way. It's kind of scary. The two of you seemed to have some special understanding that the rest of us never did." Kate shook her head in bewilderment.

With rising hope, Emily asked again if there was any chance they could keep the farm.

"I really don't see how, Em." Kate looked really sorry for the decision. "If there was a way, we'd have thought of it."

Although terribly disappointed, by now Emily was beginning to accept losing the farm. She figured if Emma's granny and the rest of her family could pull up their roots from Scotland and settle in a new country, she'd somehow have to come to terms with not being able to visit her grandparents' farm any more.

Mother and daughter strolled companionably back to the house, discussing their return to Regina on Sunday night. Emily was excited about seeing Courtney and Samantha again and everyone at school, but distressed at leaving Emma behind. She had only tomorrow to spend with her.

Aunt Liz was back from town when they returned. If she was surprised when Kate and Emily entered the house rosy and animated from their walk, she said nothing. She just gave Emily the "thumbs up" signal when Kate had her back turned. And Emily grinned.

AN EARLY LIGHT SUPPER left plenty of time for Emily to make a quick trip back to Emma's, now that the evenings were getting longer. Her mother agreed, on the condition that she be home before dark. Emily was surprised by her mother's assent, but Kate had remembered hearing about some new people on a nearby farm, and assumed this was where Emily was headed.

Emily reached the rock in record time, but found herself in a brisk wind pelted with rain when she grabbed the stone. Although she had only her sneakers on her feet, she was thankful she'd dressed warmly in a thick sweater and a jacket.

Pulling the hood over her head, she tucked her chin to her chest and ran through the trees to Emma's sod house. Once there, she noticed the flicker of a candle burning through the shutters of the window, and figured the family would be inside during the storm. Most of the family appeared to be present when she peeked inside, except for Emma's father and two of her older brothers.

Mrs. Elliott's back was to Emily. She was darning socks by the window as she rocked Molly in the cradle. When she turned her head, Emily could see lines of concern and apprehension etched on her face. The other family members seemed to be gathered around the table quietly playing cards. At times Bella or Beth checked on a lone figure lying on one of the cots. It took Emily a few moments to realize it had to be Emma.

What could be wrong with her? Emily had to have a closer look. She wiped the trickles of rain off her face, and in desperation tried to think of a way to get into the house without arousing any undue attention.

Just then Emma's father and brothers emerged from the sod barn. Buffeted by the wind, they ran across the yard. The sky lit up with lightning as they neared the woodpile, where they each gathered an armload of firewood. When they reached the house and yanked open the door, Emily was right beside them. She slipped inside when a heavy gust of wind grabbed the door from Duncan's hand. By the time he slammed it shut, she'd moved to Emma's bedside.

Her friend lay quiet and pale like a fragile porcelain doll, with her long sandy hair in matted strands on her pillow. She opened her eyes when a spasm of coughing overtook her, and for an instant she seemed to recognize Emily.

"Oh, my God. Emma, what's happened to you?" Emily whispered urgently over the clunking of wood being thrown into the wood box. She reached out and swept her hand across the girl's forehead. Emma was hot to the touch. Her breathing was strained and irregular. Emily knew she had to do something, but what?

Then Emma's mother rushed to her side and Emily stepped out of the way. She watched as Mrs. Elliott removed a cloth from the girl's chest and replaced it with another. From the acrid smell, Emily thought it must be one of the mixtures she'd taught them to make. She was pleased by this, but wondered what else were they doing for her friend.

A moment later Bella arrived by the bedside and tried to get Emma to swallow a mouthful of some tonic, but the movement of raising her head brought on an even worse spasm of coughing. As Bella laid Emma's head down on the pillow, Emma's father approached.

"How is the lass?"

"No change," his wife replied, and shook her head sadly. Gently Mr. Elliott clasped his calloused hand on Emma's shoulder, then bowed his head and moved away. Her mother pulled the covers back up to her chin and with a forlorn sigh returned to her rocking chair by the window. Bella sat for a moment at the edge of the cot, staring down at Emma.

Maybe Bella can hear me, thought Emily moving closer. She called quietly at first, but when there was no answer she shouted. No one responded, except Molly, who began whimpering. In frustration, Emily yelled as loud as she could. This caused Molly to scream. While pandemonium broke out over the baby's sudden shrieking, Emily sagged against the wall and slid to the floor. She wept quietly. She could hear the howl of the wind outside, and the drumming of the rain as it lashed against the shutter.

Fear and despair clutched at Emily. Molly was the only one who could hear her, and she couldn't communicate. Emma wasn't responding at all. A coldness crept through her body, and Emily knew it was not from being drenched and chilled in the thunderstorm. The house was exceptionally warm with all the people inside and the roaring fire from the cookstove. But Emily couldn't keep her teeth from chattering. She had never been so scared.

Suddenly Geordie volunteered to venture outside for some more medicinal plants. They were running low. "Maybe they'll help Emma," he suggested in a low voice.

Emily applauded from across the room. Yes. Maybe Geordie's plan would be the turning point. She stepped towards him, then halted when his mother rose from her seat.

"You can't go out in this, lad."

"Let him go, Margaret." Emma's father drew her back. "The thunder and lightning have stopped. He'll only get wet."

Emily could tell he thought it was a good idea for the boy to have something to do. Geordie had been the closest in age to Emma, but close in other ways too — even though he'd always teased her. As Geordie dressed for the outdoors, Emily went once more to Emma's bedside.

Gently she brushed the girl's hair from her forehead. "Everything will be all right, Emma. It just has to be." Then she bent and kissed her on the cheek. "Good-bye, dear friend." She turned and followed Geordie out the door. In her heart Emily knew there was nothing she could do.

A blast of wind took Emily's breath away as she stepped outside. The rain was coming down in torrents, and she was soaked by the time she reached the rock. She replaced the stone quickly, relieved to find the evening dry in her own world.

"THAT WAS CERTAINLY TAKING your curfew to the limit, Emily," her mother said when she returned. "And how on earth did your hair get wet? And your clothes?"

"Aw, we were having a water fight." Emily said the first thing that came into her mind. She was so upset about Emma she wasn't thinking clearly.

"Well, that wasn't a very smart thing to do. It's not that warm out there. Honestly, Em, I wonder where your common sense is sometimes." Kate shook her head in dismay. "Run up and have a hot bath. Then I'll make you some hot chocolate. Do you want it in your room, or do you want to come down for it?"

"Upstairs, please. And thanks, Mom." Emily gave Kate a smile, then plodded up the stairs. Her body felt like an icicle, and she had trouble lifting her feet. It was as if her ankles had huge stones tied to them. All she could think about was Emma. Emily prayed that her friend would be all right.

CHAPTER TEN

Wearily Emily reached for her clothes the next morning, and found them still damp from the previous night. Tossing them aside, she grabbed some clean ones from her suitcase, and staggered into them. Then, as quietly as she could, she crept down the stairs. She had to see how Emma was, no matter what.

Aunt Liz was already sitting at the kitchen table, reading a book and sipping coffee. "Well, look what the cat dragged in," she said when she caught sight of Emily in the doorway. "You look like you had a tough night, kiddo."

"Yeah, kinda," Emily answered, trying to think of a way of getting out of the house without too much fuss. The straightforward approach worked before, she decided. She'd use it again. "I guess I'm worried about Emma. She wasn't feeling too well last night. I thought I'd go and see how she was today. And we'll be leaving tonight. I may not see her again for a long time."

With a shrug of her shoulders, Aunt Liz said, "Sounds good enough for me. Sure, go ahead, Em. I'll tell your mom you'll be back soon. And you will be, right?"

"Yes, I promise." Emily gave her aunt a hug. "Thanks."

Stumbling across the pasture, Emily hardly noticed the bright turquoise sky above her. Her legs felt like wood, and the grassy hummocks beneath her clumsy feet felt more rugged than usual. It seemed to take her forever to reach the rock.

Shivering when she arrived, Emily reached into the crevice for the stone. But she couldn't feel it. She delved deeper, her fingers clawing at the inside of the crack. But she found only bits of sand. In a panic she scrambled up the face of the rock and peered into the crevice. The stone wasn't there.

Oh, no.

Emily dropped to the ground. Where could it be? Maybe she hadn't put the stone back properly the night before. Or maybe the torrents of rain had washed it out. She searched the ground. Nothing. Frantically she fell to her knees and crawled about, patting the area. In a wider arc she probed and scraped the surface with her hands, examining the same places over and over again. She didn't miss an inch.

Almost hysterical now, Emily examined the side of the rock as she climbed. She checked all the cavities where the stone could possibly fit. Then she crawled on top of the slab and felt around the flat surface, even though she could see it wasn't there. At last she sat back and rocked on her heels. The stone was gone. Tears streamed down her face. "Emma," she wailed. "Emma."

A few moments later she reeled back to her feet and slid down to the ground. She began jogging over the terrain where the bluff of poplars and the path to Emma's sod house had been a hundred years earlier. They were all gone. Yet Emily kept running, trying to imagine where the Elliotts' yard had been. She couldn't really tell; the land had changed so much since then. But perhaps the three mounds, one smaller than the others, in a flat area where she stopped had been the house, the barn, and the root cellar.

"Emma, where are you?" She called again and again as she whirled about in panic and disbelief. Finally she stood in silence, her head bowed. There was no joy at seeing the wildflowers at her feet or hearing the birds twittering overhead in the sunlight. She drew no comfort from the wind. Now she was locked out of Emma's world forever.

ALTHOUGH she trudged home some time later, she didn't recall getting there. She was too numb. Nor did Emily know how she made it through the rest of the morning or notice the worried glances exchanged between her mother and aunt. They left her alone in her attic room with her unexplained sorrow.

Emily threw herself across her bed. What had become of Emma? Would she ever know? Emma had been so sick the last time she saw her. Surely she'd recovered. Emily fell into a fitful state halfway between sleep and waking, and dreamt of Emma.

Emma as she'd seen her the first time on the rock, and later exhausted as she cared for her family. Emma picking mushrooms in the meadow, being chased by Geordie, and playing with Molly. Emma as she hugged Emily good-bye, and then discovered Geordie hiding. Emma lying ill, and Geordie going out for plants in the rain. Emma and Geordie…Geordie. His name echoed in Emily's head.

She sat up with a jolt. Geordie must have taken the stone! It made sense. He was always lurking around whenever they were at the rock. And that day when she'd seen the movement in the trees, it must have been Geordie. He must have gone back to the rock since the last time Emily had been there, and found the smooth stone. "Oh Geordie," she moaned. "You don't know what you've done."

"Emily, are you okay?" Her mother called from the bottom of the attic stairs.

"Y-yes." Emily jumped off the bed and moved to the window, hiding her face. But Kate didn't come up. "Aunt Maggie's here," she continued. "She wants to go to the cemetery right away and put some flowers on Grandma's grave. Do you want to come with us?"

"Yeah." Emily sniffled. She hadn't heard Aunt Maggie arrive, but sitting in her room moping wouldn't help her slip back in time to find Emma. She might as well go. At least she'd probably feel closer to her grandmother. "I'll be right down."

With a sudden glimmer of excitement, she realized Aunt Maggie would be able to answer her questions about their family background. If she didn't know, no one would. Emily took the stairs two at a time, stopping in the bathroom to wash her face and tie back her hair.

When they arrived at the cemetery a short time later, she tumbled out of the car ahead of the others. But then she held back. It might be more fitting to allow the others to go first. Aunt Maggie at seventy-two was the oldest of Grandma Renfrew's family, and she walked slowly on arthritic legs, using a cane for support. Emily had plenty of time to read the other headstones as they strolled along in the peaceful shade of the towering spruce. The trees had been planted around the cemetery years before. She saw some familiar names like Ferguson and Barkley, and Aunt Maggie's husband, Joseph Henderson, who had died many years before. At last they came to the Renfrew family plots.

Emily stood silently with her mother and Aunt Liz as Aunt Maggie placed the lilies by her grandparents' monument. Then she wandered off, not wanting to stand by the new mound of earth. Her grandmother's body lay there, but not her spirit. Instead, she ambled along the grassy paths as the others chatted quietly.

She examined the engravings on the headstones, discovering earlier and earlier dates. She felt herself drawn to the oldest section in a far corner of the graveyard. Here the inscriptions were more difficult to read on the weathered white stones, and some markers had fallen over.

As she paced slowly between the gravesites, studying each of them, a strange feeling of anticipation came over her. Then she found what she knew would be there: a row of Elliott family crosses. They stretched in an irregular line along the back of the cemetery. Apprehensively, she read the names.

At the very outside edge she found Granny Elliott's modest tombstone. Emily fell to her knees, shivering. Right beside it, she discovered a smaller one. She pushed aside the wild rose bushes that almost obscured the dates and read: *Emma, Beloved Daughter of George and Margaret Elliott, 5 May 1887 - 27 September 1899.*

Reaching out a shaky hand, Emily fingered the etchings on the headstone and whispered a silent prayer for her long gone friend. In her heart she'd known Emma had not survived the terrible illness. Rising and stepping away, she headed to the line of spruce trees and crawled through the fence that enclosed the cemetery. She stood breathing deeply in the warm spring sun, staring across the landscape.

She was not surprised to find that she could see the outcrop of rocks on her grandparents' farm in the distance. She knew now she was standing on the outer edge of what had been the Elliotts' property. In silence she walked back to the car where the others waited for her.

Emily felt they'd obviously been talking about her, because they fell silent when she approached. She couldn't bring herself to speak. Instead, she stared out the window at the blur of scenery that streaked past in swirls of dust as they drove along the gravel roads.

When they returned to the house, Emily shot up the stairs for the old family photograph hidden under her window ledge. She needed to find out about the people in it. Aunt Maggie was the only one who could make any connections at all.

Her mother and Aunt Liz were preparing coffee, but they stopped short when Emily thrust the photograph into her aunt's hand. All thoughts of a snack were forgotten when Aunt Maggie exclaimed in surprise at the print.

"Goodness, Emily. Where on earth did you come across this?"

Quickly she explained about finding the glass negatives in the attic and her mother getting the print made. "Do you know who they are?" Emily held her breath. She could hear the clock ticking as she waited for her aunt to answer.

"Well...." Aunt Maggie studied the photograph. "These are your relatives on your grandmother's side – the Elliotts."

So she'd been right. Her grandmother and Emma had been related. But how? "Who are they?" Emily pumped, hardly able to contain her eagerness. She pulled out a chair and sat down at the table by her aunt.

"Well, this is George Elliott Senior and his wife, Margaret," Aunt Maggie said pointing to the older couple. "They'd be your great-grandparents."

"Really? My great-grandparents?" Emily caught her breath and exhaled slowly, waiting for her aunt to confirm it.

"Certainly. They'd be your grandmother Renfrew's parents," Aunt Maggie repeated, stopping after every word as if to emphasize each generation. She tapped her fingers slowly on the table top as she thought.

"Wow." If they were her great-grandparents, then that meant Emma must be her great-aunt. A sudden giddiness swept through Emily. "But where's Grandma in the photo?"

"She wasn't even born when this picture was taken. They took this before they left Scotland. Your great-grandmother was expecting your grandmother when they decided to emigrate."

"And she was born on the wagon trail here." Emily interrupted, thoroughly excited now.

"Why yes, Emily. She was."

"Wait a minute. I thought it was Molly that was born on the trail?" Emily tilted her head and looked at Aunt Maggie. She thought hard. Something didn't fit.

Aunt Maggie chuckled. "You're partly right. Molly was what they called your grandmother when she was younger. But she was christened Mary. When she grew up, there was another Molly in the community, so she decided to switch back to Mary."

Kate looked at Emily with a puzzled expression on her face. "How did you know?"

Emily realized her mistake. She took a breath and tried to calm herself. "Uh, I guess maybe Grandma told me about it or something."

"So, can you tell us who the others are?" Aunt Liz questioned. They all gathered in closer around Aunt Maggie.

"I'm not sure I recognize everyone. When I knew them they were much older, of course. But let's see." Slowly Aunt Maggie pointed to the two youngest-looking girls. "These would be Beth and Kate — Elizabeth, no, Elsbeth, and Katherine, really." She turned to look at Emily's mother. "You knew you were named for her didn't you?"

"Yes, I did," said Kate. "Mom always said I was head-strong and stubborn, just like Auntie Kate."

"She was right." Aunt Liz stepped away as Kate tried to give her a playful swat.

"Now, girls." Aunt Maggie reprimanded them, then continued naming the faces in the photo. "These are probably Uncle Alex, and Auntie Bella. They were the oldest. I'm not sure of all the others."

"Uncle Alex — was he called Sandy?" Emily felt a faint smile tug at her mouth.

"Why yes, I believe he was — when he was a boy." Aunt Maggie turned back to pondering the photo, mumbling names to herself. "Some of them died young and some moved away. Uncle Jack was the one that died nine or ten years ago. You probably don't remember him, do you Emily?"

"Yeah, sort of. Is he the one with the big bushy eyebrows and long tickly white beard, that lived near Wolseley?"

"Wow, you do have a memory, kiddo. You'd only have been about three when he died," said Aunt Liz.

Aunt Maggie raised her eyebrows at Emily. "And this was Uncle Duncan. He's been gone for years. He left the farm and moved to Victoria after his wife Anne passed away." She paused. "Now some of these middle children I'm not sure of."

Why was she so slow to recognize them? Emily couldn't contain her excitement any longer. "That's Geordie." She pointed to him in the photo.

"Well, I believe you're right, Emily. How did you know?"

"I suppose your grandmother mentioned him too?" asked Aunt Liz, coming to her rescue.

"Yes, I guess so," said Emily, relieved she didn't have to provide an explanation.

"And this must have been Emma. Such a tragedy, you know." Aunt Maggie seemed unaware that Emily had sucked in her breath and was waiting for her to go on. "She survived a 'flu epidemic while caring for the rest of the family. In fact, they say she saved Molly and her mother from death's door. But she was so worn out, poor child, that when she caught pneumonia, she never recovered."

Emily turned to see both Kate and Aunt Liz looking at her with thoughtful expressions. She stood passively, listening to her aunt.

"There wasn't much that could be done in those days," Aunt Maggie continued. "No doctors around. And they didn't have the kinds of medication we have today. None of the rest of the family knew anything about plant medicines. What with the old Granny gone – that was George Senior's mother, you know. She died in the epidemic, a month earlier. Even if they had known what plants to use, Emma was too run-down. She wouldn't have made it anyway."

"It's too bad, really," her aunt stared at her gnarled hands. "They say Emma could have made a wonderful doctor. She had this natural ability to recognize plants and know what they were good for."

Emily smiled at this.

"Your grandmother used to say she could feel Emma around her like a guardian angel, teaching her all about nature's ways." Aunt Maggie twisted in her chair to look at Emily, and poked her in the side with her cane. "You know, young lady, your grandmother insisted you be named for Emma. As soon as you were born, she said she had the feeling you were a kindred spirit. Of course, your mother, stubborn as she is, wouldn't give in entirely. She said Emma was too old fashioned. Emily was as close to Emma as she'd allow."

Emily felt warmed by this knowledge. Grandmother Renfrew had been special to her as well. As her aunt drifted into grumbling about her various medical problems, Emily walked over to the kitchen counter and stared out the window in a daze.

"Em, are you all right?" Her mother came up behind her.

"Yes. I was just thinking about what it must have been like for Grandma's family…being pioneers." She turned back to the table and picked the photo up again. Gently she caressed the picture with her fingertips. "So, this is the Elliott family then. And that's Grandmother's parents and brothers and sisters."

Kate placed a hand on Emily's shoulder, just as Aunt Liz came up behind them. "That's quite a story about Emma," her aunt remarked. "I remember hearing something about her when I was a child."

"Yes," agreed her mother. "And isn't it strange that you just met someone named Emma too, Em?"

Emily nodded and didn't respond, hoping there would be no more questions. Instead she pictured Emma standing on the rock the first day she'd seen her with her apron and blue-flowered dress blowing in the wind. All of a sudden Emily remembered Grandmother Renfrew's quilt. "Mom, could I go get that quilt and show it to Aunt Maggie? You know, the first one Grandma made?"

"Sure, Em. Do you need help getting it down?"

"No, I can manage." Emily was already on her way up the stairs. Now that she knew Emma's family was really her grandmother Renfrew's family, the coverlet had more meaning for her.

When it was laid out on the table, Emily examined the different coloured patches of material a little more closely, trying to figure out which swatches belonged to what articles of clothing. The plaids and stripes were obviously from the men's flannel shirts, and the plain and print calico bits from skirts and blouses. But what caught Emily's interest were the flowered scraps that had originally been dresses. Somewhere in a hidden corner of her mind an idea popped forward. Yes. There it was. The swatch from Emma's dress; a blue background with small pink flowers. The one Emma had always worn.

Suddenly everything was coming together for Emily, and she needed to be alone to sort it all out. "Mom would you mind if I went up to the rock one more time?"

Kate looked at her daughter, a softness about her eyes. "Sure, go ahead, Em. Say good-bye to Emma."

Emily almost blurted out that Emma was already gone, but something told her that her mother knew.

"What is this rock?" Aunt Maggie quizzed as Emily started towards the hallway for her jacket.

Kate explained the place to her, and Emily stopped to listen.

Aunt Maggie snorted. "That rock. Your Grandmother spent more time out there..." she shook her head. "I guess it was Emma's favourite place, too. That's why the area is still the way it was so long ago. No one wanted to disturb it. They sort of left it in memory of her."

"I'm glad they did. It's my favourite place too," Emily said.

Her mother looked across the room at Emily. "Em, what were you saying about that rock the other day...?"

Emily could feel the panic rising from her stomach. Oh, no. But then the kettle began whistling and Kate hurried to the stove. Emily made a beeline for the stairs. "I just have to run up to the attic for a minute."

"Would you mind putting the quilt back, Em, before you leave?" Kate called, busy pouring water into the teapot with her one good hand.

"Okay."

When she returned the quilt, Emily headed to her attic room. She wanted to jot down the dates from

Emma's headstone before she forgot them. She'd bring everything else up to date later.

In her hurry in reaching for her journal under the hidden ledge, Emily pushed the notebook farther back and felt it slide down the wall. Now how would she get it out? Sticking her hand into the gap, she dug deeper. Then her hand touched something soft and lumpy. Once over her initial fright, she tugged at the mound until it came loose.

She gasped at the sight of Emma's embroidered bag. Pulling the cords apart, she dumped the contents onto her lap. The stones! Quickly she counted them and found all ten there, including the one she'd used. She recognized its smooth oval shape.

How incredible for her grandmother to have kept them all these years! But how had Emily's special one come to be there? Had Geordie somehow realized it belonged in Emma's pouch and returned it? Perhaps that was one mystery she'd never solve.

Carefully Emily tucked the stones back into the bag and returned it to the hiding spot. There was no point in returning to the past now that Emma was gone. Jotting down the dates from the headstones in her retrieved notebook, she replaced it in the hidden wall space as well and trotted back down to the kitchen.

As she passed the table, she grabbed a sandwich, but dropped it when Aunt Maggie tapped her hand.

"Watch your manners, young lady," she said as Emily felt her face turn hot with embarrassment. "Oh, go on. Take it, now that you've touched it."

Then Emily saw the twinkle in the older lady's eyes.

"I was young once too," she observed with a wry smile.

Emily snatched it up again and turned to the window at the sound of a vehicle driving into the yard. Gerald Ferguson stepped out of his half-ton and sauntered over to the door. He never seemed to be in a hurry.

"Good day," he said, removing his cap and stepping inside when he found his knock answered immediately. "I'm glad to see you're all here. I wanted to talk a little business."

He settled into a chair and sat silent for a few moments as if collecting his thoughts. Then in his slow, purposeful manner, he told them he'd been talking to the manager at the Credit Union the day before. "I thought about what you suggested, Kate," he nodded at her, "and I talked it over with the wife — and if you people could hold off until fall, I'd like to buy the farm."

Emily widened her eyes and stared at her mother as Mr. Ferguson continued. A faint smile crossed Kate's face, and Aunt Liz winked at Emily. When Emily started to say something to her mother, Kate held a finger up to her lips.

Listening quietly, Emily felt relief flood through her. Although the aunts and Emily's mother would have to check with the other family members who had inherited it jointly, they were sure this would be agreeable.

Emily barely took note of the discussion that followed between her mother and aunts. But she did hear them mention something about saving a great deal in advertising and inconvenience, even though they would still go ahead with the auction. It seemed Gerald Ferguson didn't need any of the equipment.

Nor would he and his family take over the old stone house, because they'd just built a new one on their home place. Emily was ecstatic when he proposed that any time any of Mary Renfrew's family wanted, they were welcome to come and stay at their old home.

Emily would still be able to visit the farm and wander over the prairie to her favourite rock! She felt a smile break out on her face. She darted across the room to hug her mother. Kate smiled and hugged her back. Emily's heart lightened as she bounced out the door and headed to the pasture.

The sun streamed through wisps of clouds illuminating the meadow in brilliant colours. A scattering of crocuses still dotted the landscape amid hundreds of dandelions and the small white flowers of early field chickweed. As she strolled along her favourite grassy path, Emily tried imitating the songs of the red-winged blackbirds and yellow warblers that flitted past her. She stopped often, wanting to remember every moment of this walk. She couldn't believe her good fortune.

Although she was devastated because Emma had died and there was no longer any reason to shift back to the past, Emily was thrilled that she'd still be able to visit the farm.

Once she arrived at the rock, Emily stood back and gazed at its grandeur for a few moments. Carefully she scaled the back side and tiptoed across the top ledge. She sat, allowing her legs to dangle over the side, and felt the wind gently lift her hair. Then she closed her eyes until she felt an inner calm.

Around her she sensed the warm presence of a smiling older woman and a laughing young girl, together for all time. And Emily knew that if the farm was gone for good some day, the memories and feelings she had experienced here were locked forever in her heart. And if she ever felt lonely or needed solace, all she had to do was return to her beloved prairie.

Slipping back down, Emily hugged the rock one last time. Then she headed for home as a meadowlark sang its flute-like tune nearby. And the wind sighed as if it too were saying good-bye.

ABOUT THE AUTHOR

JUDITH SILVERTHORNE is the author of five previous books, including the sequel to this one, *The
Secret of the Stone House*, which was a finalist for
the Saskatchewan Book Award for Children's
Literature in 2005. The books in her Dinosaur
series, *Dinosaur Hideout, Dinosaur Breakout,* and
Dinosaur Steakout, have also been listed for several awards.

Judith Silverthorne works as a writer, film
producer, and cultural administrator in Regina.
For more information on Judith and her work,
consult her Web site at: *www.judithsilverthorne.ca.*

FROM MANY PEOPLES

Coteau Books began to develop the *From Many Peoples* series of novels for young readers over a year ago, as a celebration of Saskatchewan's Centennial. We looked for stories that would illuminate life in the province from the viewpoints of young people from different cultural groups and we're delighted with the stories we found.

We're especially happy with the unique partnership we have been able to form with the LaVonne Black Memorial Fund in support of *From Many Peoples*. The Fund was looking for projects it could support to honour a woman who had a strong interest in children and their education, and decided that the series was a good choice. With their help, we are able to provide free books to every school in the province, tour the authors across the province, and develop additional materials to support schools in using *From Many Peoples* titles.

This partnership will bring terrific stories to young readers all over Saskatchewan, honour LaVonne Black and her dedication to the children of this province, and help us celebrate Saskatchewan's Centennial. Thank you to everyone involved.

Nik Burton
Managing Editor, Coteau Books

LAVONNE BLACK

My sister LaVonne was born in Oxbow, Saskatchewan, and grew up on a small ranch near North-gate. She spent a lot of time riding horses and always had a dog or a cat in her life. LaVonne's favourite holiday was Christmas. She loved to sing carols and spoil children with gifts. People were of genuine interest to her. She didn't care what you did for a living, or how much money you made. What she did care about was learning as much about you as she could in the time she had with you.

We are proud of our LaVonne, a farm girl who started school in a one-room schoolhouse and later presented a case to the Supreme Court of Canada. Her work took her all over Saskatchewan, and she once said that she didn't know why some people felt they had to go other places, because there is so much beauty here. LaVonne's love and wisdom will always be with me. She taught me that what you give of yourself will be returned to you, and that you should love, play, and live with all your heart.

LaVonne felt very strongly about reading and education, and the LaVonne Black Memorial Fund and her family hope that you enjoy this series of books.

Trevor L. Black, little brother
Chair, LaVonne Black Memorial Fund

LAVONNE BLACK was a tireless advocate for children in her years with the Saskatchewan School Boards Association. Her dedication, passion, and commitment were best summed up in a letter she wrote to boards of education one month before her death, when she announced her decision to retire:

"I thank the Association for providing me with twenty-three years of work and people that I loved. I was blessed to have all that amid an organization with a mission and values in which I believed. School trustees and the administrators who work for them are special people in their commitment, their integrity, and their caring. I was truly blessed and am extremely grateful for the opportunities and experiences I was given."

LaVonne was killed in a car accident on July 19, 2003. She is survived by her daughter, Jasmine, and her fiancé, Richard. We want so much to thank her for all she gave us. Our support for this book series, *From Many Peoples,* is one way to do this. Thank you to everyone who has donated to her Memorial Fund and made this project possible.

Executive, Staff, and member boards of
The Saskatchewan School Boards Association

Also available in the series

FROM MANY PEOPLES

THE SECRET OF THE STONE HOUSE

by Judith Silverthorne

Emily Bradford time-travels to her own family's past,
and helps her ancestors settle into their new pioneer life
in Saskatchewan.

ISBN: 978-1-55050-325-8 – $8.95CAD/$7.95USD

NETTIE'S JOURNEY

by Adele Dueck

Nettie's story of life in a Mennonite village in Ukraine as told to her
granddaughter in present-day Saskatchewan. From the dangers of WWI
to their escape to Canada, this is a captivating eye-witness account
of a turbulent period in history.

ISBN: 978-1-55050-322-7 – $8.95CAD/$7.95USD

ADELINE'S DREAM

by Linda Aksomitis

Adeline has to struggle to make a place for herself when she comes to
Canada from Germany. Life in her new home is definitely dramatic, but by
Christmas time she starts to feel a sense of belonging in her new home.

ISBN: 978-1-55050-323-4 – $8.95CAD/$7.95USD

Available at fine bookstores everywhere.

COTEAU
BOOKS
FOR KIDS